HOT JOCKS 7

TAKING
HIS SHOT

New York Times & *USA Today* Bestselling Author

KENDALL RYAN

ABOUT THE BOOK

She says she doesn't date players.

She swears up and down that she'll never handle my stick.

We'll see about that, sweetheart.

When I win the pleasure of Harper's company at a charity auction, I get exactly one date—one shot to win over the gorgeous and feisty brunette.

Game on. I play hard, and I love a challenge.

But just when I think I've finally carved out my shot . . . a huge secret implodes around us, threatening everything we've built.

PLAYLIST

"Trouble" by Cage the Elephant

"Under Your Skin" by Milfy Cougar

"Like That" by Bea Miller

"Standing in the Middle of the Field" by Cut Copy

"Never Be Like You" by Flume

"Bad Guy" by Billie Eilish

"The High Road" by Broken Bells

"Slide" by Calvin Harris

"Wait" by Maroon 5

CHAPTER ONE

Never Freaking Again

Harper

"You'd tell me if I looked like a marshmallow, right?" I scrunch my nose in the mirror at the tulle monstrosity I'm wearing before turning to give my dad a worried look.

"You look great, sweetheart," he says gruffly, glancing up at me from the sports section of the newspaper that's holding his attention.

It's not like I *want* to be wearing a knee-length, skintight, pale-blue satin dress with six inches of white tulle along the hem, which makes me look like some kind of snowman-mermaid hybrid. But when your dad tells you that this year's Seattle Ice Hawks ice princess is bedridden with mono, and he begs you to step in as her replacement, you don't have that many options.

What was I supposed to do, tell him to ask his *other* daughter, who just happens to be reliably free on a Friday evening? I had no choice but to agree to help him out. Even if that means betraying one of my most sacred principles—that I will never, under any circumstances, date a hockey player.

It's specific, I know, but trust me. Growing up with a hockey coach for a father, I have my reasons. Thankfully, I'm not being auctioned off for a real date. It's just for charity.

"Listen," Dad says, rubbing the bridge of his nose and folding the paper neatly in front of him. "It's for charity. You're doing a good thing. I really appreciate you taking one for the team."

Taking one for the team. If I had a dollar for every time I've heard that phrase throughout my life . . . Well, let's just say I wouldn't be writing for an online magazine. I'd own the whole damn publishing conglomerate.

A string quartet starts playing in the distance, our cue to leave my makeshift changing room and enter the ballroom with the rest of the guests. Dad was already milling around during the cocktail hour in the foyer when I frantically texted him to come help me, and I know better than anyone that every minute spent in here with me is a minute spent not raising money for the local children's hospital.

For the record, I have nothing against charity. I think it's great what the team's doing for those kids. It's the whole *being an item in the auction* thing I'm not so thrilled about. "Win a Date with the Seattle Ice Hawks Ice Princess" is how the event is being publicized, but the real ice princess is down for the count, so I guess they're stuck with a loud-mouthed online columnist instead. Oh, and don't worry—the event organizers are still making me wear the ice princess dress, and let's just say it wasn't made for asses like mine. *Good times.*

My dad stands and straightens his tie, then adjusts his black slacks around his waist.

"You look really nice, Dad," I say, unable to stifle the smile stretching across my face.

He always wears a suit to events like this, as well as to the games, but I happen to know this suit is special. It's about as old as I am, but until recently, it hadn't fit him for about a decade.

After our mom walked out when I was little, he was so focused on taking care of me and my sister, Faith, he stopped taking care of himself—to the point that his doctor put him on heart medication two months ago. And said that if Dad didn't make some serious lifestyle changes, he'd be at serious risk for a heart attack.

Faith and I have slowly started introducing healthier options into his diet and encouraging him to get in a few hours of exercise a week. It's been an uphill battle, for sure, but he's made some real progress. And that classic, well-tailored suit he's wearing tonight is proof.

"Thanks, sweetheart. Don't hide in here for too long, okay?"

I fake a scandalized look, placing my hand on my chest and raising my eyebrows. Dad chuckles and slips out the door, the music swelling and falling as it closes.

Turning back to my reflection, I tug at the hem of the dress, but it doesn't change anything. It is what it is at this point. At least they let me wear my hair how I like it, instead of forcing it into the painful updo the ice princess normally wears. I give myself one last hopeful grin in the mirror before slinging my small beaded purse strap over my shoulder and unleashing myself on the party.

My first order of business? Find the bar. It might not be very princess-like, but zero fucks are being given. If I'm expected to be a walking, talking marshmallow, then I'm going to be a tipsy one.

As I march down the hallway in these ridiculously high strappy silver heels, the music and the murmurs of the crowd grow louder. When I turn the corner, I'm instantly greeted by a series of gasps from a group of older women to my right, who can clearly tell I'm not the real ice princess.

Flashing them my most beauty-pageant-worthy smile, I take a sharp left, scanning the ballroom for something, *anything*, to drink. It doesn't take long for my gaze to land on the bar in the far corner . . .

And the line that's twenty people deep, and growing.

Cursing under my breath, I make my way to the end of the line, wishing it was socially acceptable to ignore everyone and stare at my phone all night. How else am I supposed to deal with the awkwardness of being alone at a charity gala, wearing a dress that screams, *yes, actually, I* will *be performing at a child's birthday party after this.*

"Are you Harper Allen?" A small woman with curly red hair and horn-rimmed glasses taps me on the shoulder, looking at me expectantly over her glasses.

"Um, yes?" I say, more a question than I meant

for it to be.

"You're late. Come with me."

She grabs my wrist with her bony fingers and leads me across the ballroom, where a small crowd of people have begun to trickle in, most of them fawning over the horde of hockey players in the corner. It's easy to spot them—they stand nearly a head taller than everyone else in the room, and have wide shoulders and powerful builds.

It takes every bone in my body not to roll my eyes at the sight of them in their slick blue suits, their hair perfectly coiffed for the cameras. They're all laughing at something one of them has said, elbowing one another and slapping each other's shoulders. Cocky pricks. They think they're practically God's gift to humanity, and the worst part is, just about everyone here agrees with them.

"Um, excuse me, but where are we going?" I ask as the woman continues to lead me by the wrist, weaving through the tables covered with white tablecloths like we're competing in some timed obstacle course.

"Backstage. Auction items were supposed to be checked in twenty minutes ago. You're late."

I flinch at being referred to as an auction item,

just in time for the woman to turn and give me a disapproving glare. Seriously, my dad owes me big-time for this.

We weave around a few more tables before arriving at the stage. A tall wooden lectern stands stage left, and along the back is a single row of tables featuring posters advertising each of the items up for auction.

There's the standard VIP season ticket package, a trip to Mexico, a subscription to a fancy wine-of-the-month club—you know, the usual. And then, of course, there's the big-ticket item, the one that's been drawing crowds since the Ice Hawks Gala began: One Night of Bliss with the Seattle Ice Princess. The poster at the end depicts a staged photo with last year's princess and winner. Her smile is so blindingly white, it's almost hard to look at, while the tall man next to her looks like he might have had a few teeth replaced over the years.

It's not mandatory that one of the players wins the date every year, but it's expected that they make a real go at bidding to win. Not only does it look good for the team to have their golden boys give the appearance that they really care about sick kids, but it also encourages all the other men in the audience to compete with them, because who doesn't want their ego stroked by beating one of the Seattle Ice Hawks at winning the girl? The other bidders might not be able to outskate the players on the rink, but maybe they can outbid one of them for a date. Ridiculous, I know.

The woman drags me behind the curtain, where the certificates and gift baskets are all waiting to be put on display. I may be the only living auction item, but the way this woman starts prodding and poking at me sure doesn't make me feel human.

"Well," she says after a few minutes of fluffing the tulle around my knees, "you're no ice princess, but you'll have to do."

"I never claimed to be one, but by all means, insult away," I mutter under my breath. Clearly not under my breath enough, because the woman clucks her tongue and adjusts her glasses.

"You go onstage when you hear your item called. Smile and wave like you're sitting on a float at the Macy's Thanksgiving Day Parade. A lot of girls would kill to be in your position tonight. And stop making that face like you just stepped in dog poop."

With that, she scurries away, leaving me alone with the other pretty packages up for bids.

I take a few slow, deep breaths to calm the small fire of rage burning in my belly, reminding myself that I don't worship the team like these people do. Of course, I'm grateful for the opportunities my dad's job has given me. I'm aware that not every girl my age gets to attend fancy galas and hang out with professional athletes on any given night.

But it would be a whole lot easier to be happy about my current situation if I wasn't forced to pretend to be something I'm not. And if there wasn't a good chance I was about to be sold into a romantic evening with a freaking hockey player, which happens to be my least favorite brand of human.

I usually date hipster types, the kind of guys who appreciate poetry and obscure web comics, someone who wouldn't know what to do with a hockey stick if his life depended on it. Someone who sure as hell wouldn't prioritize a silly game over *me*.

Been there. Done that. And I have the emotional scars to prove it.

The music dies down, and the crowd erupts into a round of applause, which almost certainly means that my father is walking onto the stage to give his speech. While I've never heard it live, he's rehearsed it enough at home that I practically know it by heart. He'll thank everyone for being here to-night, talk about the important work the children's hospital does, how meaningful their partnership is with the team, *blah, blah, blah*. It's sweet, it's touching, and it's everything it needs to be to make these rich donors open their hearts—and more importantly, their wallets.

Dad delivers it perfectly, landing every joke (which I wrote for him, of course), and receives the appropriate murmurs of solidarity at the *tug on your heartstrings* parts. My heart swells with pride when I hear the loud applause that follows him off-stage. These kinds of events aren't why he got into this business, but damn, is he good at them.

Dad is replaced onstage by the auctioneer of the night, a tall man in a shiny silver suit who introduc-es himself as Stan. By the time he gets through his introductory remarks, I'm tuning him out, my ears ringing and my knees going weak at the thought of getting up on that stage.

For some reason, it didn't quite hit me until this moment that I'm going to have to stand there in front of hundreds of people, in this ridiculous dress, for however long it takes for the bidding to be over. My head starts to spin and I'm about to look for somewhere to sit down when I hear the words I've been dreading this entire night.

"And now, the moment you've all been waiting for. Please welcome the Seattle Ice Hawks ice princess!"

I take a deep breath and climb the small set of stairs onto the stage, plastering the biggest pageant smile I can muster on my face, and march confidently to my mark to the right of the podium. The lights are bright, and I do my best not to squint as my eyes take longer than I'd like to adjust.

"How are you doing this evening, darlin'?" Stan drawls, holding the mic in front of my face.

"I'm wonderful, Stan, thank you for asking," I reply in a sugary-sweet voice.

Sitting at one of the tables near the front, the woman in horn-rimmed glasses gives me an approving nod. Even I'm surprised by how confident and at ease I sound.

"Well, Princess, you're about to be even better. Because tonight, one of these handsome men in the audience will win the opportunity to take you out!"

The crowd cheers, and I smile graciously at them in mock excitement, giving them the biggest smile I can muster, even winking for good measure.

Honestly? I might be dying inside, but on the outside, I'm killing this shit. Maybe if writing doesn't work out, I could consider the pageant circuit.

"Let's say we start the bidding at one hundred dollars. Come on, boys, one hundred dollars, one hundred dollars, do I see one fifty? One fifty! Two hundred dollars, she's quite a looker, fellas . . ."

The bidding process hurtles on so quickly, I can hardly keep track of the paddle-waving hands shooting up into the air, and I give up on trying to see who's bidding. There are way more of them than I ever expected.

In some ways, it's flattering to see so many men vying for the chance to take you out on a date, but I know that it's a pissing contest more than anything. It's not really about me or who I am as a person; it's about showing all the other guys how much cash you can shell out in one night, and being the lucky asshole to land the ice princess. Still, I can't keep my stomach from flip-flopping with every paddle that flies into the air, the same thought bouncing around and around inside my head.

Please not a hockey player, please not a hockey player, please not a hockey player . . .

"Sold! For one thousand dollars to the man in

the blue tie. Come on up here, son, and tell us your name."

Stan claps, and the crowd instantly joins in the applause.

I've been so lost in my own anxiety, I didn't see the final bid, so I frantically scan the crowd to find the guy who's just purchased me. Squinting into the audience, I catch the eye of the woman in the horn-rimmed glasses, who gives me a sharp look and raises her clapping hands to prompt me. A little too late, I join in on the applause as well, just as I spot a broad-shouldered form rising from the players' table.

Shit, shit, shit.

You've gotta be freaking kidding me.

The man rapidly approaching the stage is a player, all right, with his wide shoulders, powerful thick thighs, and his unruly hair pushed artfully off his face.

I don't recognize him, but that doesn't mean much. I stopped paying attention to my dad's team the second I stopped living under his roof. Hell, I couldn't even come up with a single name from the pool of his highest-paid stars in the last ten years, let alone from his current roster.

The crowd erupts in another loud cheer as the man reaches the stage, taking the short flight of stairs with such ease, you'd think he was skating on ice. He greets Stan with a firm, boisterous handshake before turning and flashing me a kind, winning smile. I steel myself and smile back, but I know this one doesn't meet my eyes. Even though I might not know anything about this guy, I do know his type.

Sure, he's gorgeous, with blue eyes so pretty, I forget my own name for a second. And, yes, that smile made my heart do a roundoff back handspring. But I can guarantee that he's convinced he's the best thing since sliced bread, and if it came down to it, he wouldn't think twice about choosing his career and his team over me.

I've spent my whole life watching player after player cycle through their pick of hockey groupies, dropping them without a second thought when their relationship was "pulling focus from the team." These guys are selfish and sweaty and loud and rough. And I can guarantee this one is no different.

"What's your name, son?" Stan asks, holding the mic in front of the winner's face.

"Jordan Prescott," he says, taking the mic in

his hand. He then turns to me, his full mouth lifting, and gazes at me with a curious expression that sends a tingle between my legs.

Stupid pheromones.

"But you can call me Jordie."

The team hoots and hollers as the crowd laughs with delight. Jordie smiles at me again, and this time, I smile back with the same level of confidence and ease.

Have your fun now, Jordan Prescott, because there's no way in hell we're ever going on a date.

CHAPTER TWO

It's Go Time, Baby

Jordie

"**Y**ou are such a dumb fuck," my teammate Teddy says with a laugh. "Shit, this is gold."

Sliding into my seat, I grab the pint glass in front of me and take a long gulp of beer while I wait for the laughter coming from my teammates to subside.

My prize, the ice princess, has been escorted backstage for who knows what, so I've rejoined my teammates at the table—my teammates who are all currently making fun of me. *Fuckers.*

"Why's that?" I ask. It's tradition for the rookies on the team to bid on the ice princess, and I'm not one to buck tradition. I'm damn happy to have a spot on this team's roster, and I'm not about to fuck it up by breaking protocol.

"Because that hot little number you just bid on?" Teddy says with a sly smile that lights up his entire face. "Is Coach Allen's daughter."

Shit. That little bombshell settles like a hockey puck in the pit of my stomach, but a quick glance over at Coach Allen reassures me the slightest bit. He's seated with the team leadership with a huge grin on his face.

He knows it's a tradition for one of the guys to take her out, so he must be cool with it. *Right?* Mark Allen only joined the coaching staff this past year, so I'm still learning about what sets him off, but me bidding on his daughter doesn't seem to be one of them.

"He doesn't seem too bent out of shape about it," I say, casually taking another sip of my beer.

Morgan, our backup goalie, leans back, crossing his bulky forearms over his chest. "You do realize you can't hook up with her once and never call her again. Not unless you want to kiss your career good-bye."

I scowl at him. "Who says I'm going to do that?"

Yeah, I might have a growing reputation for casual hookups. But that doesn't mean that's all I'm looking for, despite what the guys around me obviously think.

"So, what, are you going to *date* her? You looking for monogamy now, rookie?" Morgan chuckles into his beer like that's the funniest thing he's heard all day.

Straightening, I shoot him a pointed look. "Maybe I am." Hell, I don't know. She is hot as fuck.

"Jordie, let's think about this for a second. You've never had a serious girlfriend, and you're what . . . twenty-six years old?"

"Twenty-five," I say, narrowing my eyes at him. "So what?"

I'm young, and I've enjoyed playing the field. It doesn't mean I'm *never* going to settle down. These guys should understand that better than anyone. Hell, most of them were huge man-whores before settling down with their current wives and girlfriends. Hypocritical much?

"So . . . you going after Harper Allen makes about as much sense as a grizzly bear dating a ladybug," Teddy says to another chorus of laughter.

"You want some aloe, rookie? You just got burned." Morgan chuckles into his fist.

"Having her in my bed every night wouldn't exactly be a hardship now, would it?" I say, and the guys shrug. *One point, Jordie.*

"There's just one tiny problem with that plan," Teddy says.

"You mean other than her being Coach's daughter?"

"Yeah," he says, and all the guys laugh like they know something I don't.

"She doesn't date players," Justin, our starting center, says over the rim of his glass.

"What do you mean?"

He shrugs. "Just a rumor buzzing around. She's turned down every single guy who's asked, and she's made them very well aware that they'll never have a chance with her, no matter how hard they try."

"Well, she does now," I say with a cocky smirk.

Morgan's jaw flexes with an amused smile. "Someone's overly confident."

"How could you say no to this face?" I flash

them a cocksure grin.

Morgan rolls his eyes. "Care to place a wager on that?"

"You know I never back down from a challenge. What'd you have in mind?"

"A bet. Winner takes all. We just need to decide the stakes."

"I'm game."

"You guys are idiots," Teddy says with a shake of his head.

Morgan leans forward, placing his elbows on the table as he meets my gaze with a determined expression. One problem about hanging out with hockey players—they're competitive as fuck—myself included. "A thousand bucks says you can't get Harper Allen to fall for you."

"Oh, you're on." This is going to be the easiest money I've ever made. Getting girls to fall for me has never been an issue before. Why should this one be any different?

"We need to put a timetable on this," Morgan says. "One month? Two? What do you say?"

"One. Easy. Watch and learn, boys." I rise to

my feet and head toward Harper, who's just appeared from backstage.

Harper is five and half feet of curves, with long dark hair, big brown eyes that sparkle with intelligence and wit, and a perky ass I want to bite into. In a word, she's stunning. Looks wise, I'd peg her as a younger Jessica Biel—confident, outspoken, intelligent, and gorgeous.

She's standing in line at the bar when I approach, looking like she's getting more pissed off with every second that passes.

"Hey," I say, stopping beside her with a confident smile. My fingers itch with the urge to reach out and run one palm along her spine, but I shove my hands into my pockets instead. *One thing at time, Jordie.*

Harper flashes me a quick, annoyed look, then mutters something under her breath I can't make out as she turns back toward the bar.

"Having fun?" I ask.

She releases a slow, agitated exhale. "What's a girl got to do to get a drink around here?"

Waving over a server who's circling the room with a tray of hors d'oeuvres, I slip him a crisp hundred-dollar bill. He can't be older than nineteen or twenty, and his eyes widen as he accepts the tip.

"Do me a favor and get a drink for the lady?"

He nods enthusiastically. "Absolutely, sir."

I turn to Harper. "What would you like?" I anticipate she's going to order a white wine, or maybe a glass of champagne, but Harper surprises me.

She addresses the server directly, not bothering to even look in my direction. "A gin and tonic. Hendrick's, if you have it, with cucumber, not lime."

Fuck, she's perfect.

Less than a minute later, the server reappears with her drink, along with a fresh beer for me.

"Better?" I ask as she accepts the tall glass and lifts it to her lips.

"I'm supposed to be impressed because you have money?" she says with a biting tone and a roll of her eyes.

My mouth twitches with a smile. I love a feisty girl who makes me work for it. "I think the words you're looking for are *thank you, Jordie.*"

She scoffs, rolling her eyes again, and then takes a long sip of her gin and tonic. My brain momentarily short-circuits, and I forget how to breathe as her lips wrap around the straw. She's that pretty.

Her eyes are arresting and moody, and I like them way too much. The deep-seated desire to know what makes her tick thrums steadily just beneath the surface. I'm intrigued, and I haven't been intrigued by a woman in a long-ass time. Random hookups with girls I won't remember, maybe a quick b-job in the bathroom … those are more my style, and for the record, I'm not proud of it. But something about Harper has me curious, and I want to know more.

"Bad time of the month?" I blurt.

Her jaw tics and fire burns in her eyes. "Did you seriously just imply that I'm suffering from PMS?"

I shrug and take a sip of beer before I respond. "I just figure it's possible your poor mood is due in part to the shedding of your uterine lining. I've read that can be a particularly unpleasant time of the month for a woman."

I'm hoping to make her laugh with my ridiculous statement, but Harper doesn't smile. Her lips don't even twitch, but her eyes sure do narrow at me. She looks irritated as fuck.

"You're unreal, you know that?"

"Thanks." I grin at her, shoving one hand in my pocket.

She wrinkles her nose at me and shakes her head in exasperation, like she's dealing with a disobedient child. Even that is hot. "It wasn't a compliment."

I straighten my shoulders, my mouth turning down. "Listen, I apologize if we got off on the wrong foot. Can we start over?"

"I—" She opens her mouth, probably to refuse my request, or maybe to tell me to fuck off.

But I'm faster than she is, and I don't give her the chance to shoot me down.

"Thank God," I say. "Because I'm afraid I just came across as a total douche."

"A douche?" She blinks at me, and I nod.

"Can I tell you a secret?"

Exasperated now, she sighs. "If you must."

I scan the room before looking back at her. "I hate these things."

"You hate charity?" She smiles crookedly, obviously pleased that I've just shoved my foot in my mouth.

"No. The charity aspect, I'm cool with. But I don't like all the rest of it—wearing a tux, making small talk, the tiny appetizers."

Working her bottom lip between her teeth, Harper shifts. "How can you hate those little fig-and-brie things? They were heaven. Did you even have one?"

I frown. "Damn. I missed those."

Harper chuckles, clearly pleased by my obvious disappointment at having missed out. The sound of her laugh is deep and husky and so perfect, it sends little fractures of heat zipping down my spine.

"You know what I think?" I say, gazing down at her. Even though she's wearing heels, I tower over her. Rubbing one hand over the stubble on my jaw, I lock my gaze with hers. Her expression is bored, uninterested, but her chest rises as she draws a steadying breath.

"What do you think, Jordie?" She meets my eyes. "Please enlighten me."

God, the sound of my name from her mouth. "I think you hate these things too."

Her expression softens, and her eyes move from mine to my mouth and back again. "Do you want the truth?"

Nodding, I encourage her. "Of course. Give it to me straight."

She takes another long sip of her drink, momentarily stalling. Her lips are full and kissable, but I force my gaze away because the sudden tightening in my balls pulls my attention south.

"I don't hate these events. I hate hockey players. So you might as well give up now, because you've got no chance."

"Hate is a very strong word." I clutch my chest in mock discomfort, rubbing the spot over my heart. I don't miss the way her gaze tracks hotly over my chest, and my mouth twitches as I suppress a smile.

"Well, it's a strong dislike then. Which means you're barking up the wrong tree, because this"— she waves a finger between us—"won't happen. I'm not interested, and I never will be, so you might as well just run along and find a willing participant to have your fun with. A puck bunny will fit the bill, I'm sure." She finishes this little monologue with a confident smile.

A husky chuckle falls from my mouth. "I don't believe that for a second. But enjoy your drink. See you soon, Harper."

I know how to quit when I'm ahead, and based on how little Miss Cranky Pants ogled my chest, I know I've gotten under her skin. That's all I need for tonight. She'll be screaming out my name in no time.

Watch and learn, boys.

CHAPTER THREE

Brain Versus Beauty

Harper

Y ou know what I've never really understood? How two hours at these charity events feels like forty freaking days and nights.

Oh, and that Jordie guy? Predictable as hell. I'm talking, like, textbook hockey player. Cocky, self-absorbed, and just my luck, unbearably good-looking.

I've had a good bit of practice turning down stick-swinging assholes, but it's been a while since one of them has thrown me off my game like that. Not that it changes anything. When it comes down to it, Jordie's just like the rest of them—totally not worth the time or effort. And once I send him packing, I'm sure he'll just move on to the next girl.

Scanning the slowly emptying ballroom, I spot

my dad across the way, shaking hands with a few of his players. Of course, Jordie is with them, but I do my best to ignore him. My feet are killing me and my head is throbbing, and all I need to be free to leave is my dad's nod of approval.

Good-bye, Ice Princess. Hello, Studio Apartment Hobbit. My ratty, most comfortable sweatpants and oversized hoodie await.

Finally, my dad looks up, and I rub my right earlobe, a signal that's part of the family secret code we developed when my sister and I were kids. This signal means *I'm ready to get the heck out of here.*

He grins, clapping one of his players on the back while subtly rubbing his nose, another signal in the family secret code. But this is the one I don't want to see. It means *Oh, come on. Five more minutes.*

Making the kind of sour face that would surely get an ice princess fired, I rub my earlobe even harder. Too hard, probably, given the funny looks I get from a couple walking past me. But I don't care.

I did my part. I grinned. I bore it. I wore the dress. And now I want *out.*

With a reluctant look, my dad sighs and nods toward the door. I do a secret happy dance on the inside, blowing him a kiss before bolting for the makeshift changing room down the hall.

Once in the room, I shimmy out of the dress, taking my first deep breath in hours as the restrictive fabric releases my body. Let's just say I won't be wearing satin again for a long, long time.

I slip into my jeans and a floral cotton top, and hang the monstrosity of a dress back up. Giving it one last fluff around the hem, I say a little prayer for the next girl who wears it. Hopefully, they'll have better luck than I did tonight.

After gathering the rest of my things, I march through the lobby with my head lowered, avoiding eye contact with any of the gala-goers. The last thing I need is for any one of these people to recognize me and ask where the ice princess is hurrying off to before ten p.m.

Just as I slip through the revolving doors, my fingers itching for the cool leather of my steering wheel, a voice stops me. A familiar voice. One I wasn't hoping to hear again anytime soon.

"Did you think I was going to let you sneak out of here without setting a date?"

I turn around to find Jordie standing there with that same charming smile on his face. At this point, I'm about ready to slap it right off him.

"It's not like you won my hand in marriage," I say, my tone more hostile than even I was expecting.

He's not thrown off, though. If anything, he smiles wider.

"Don't count me out yet, princess. Maybe after our one night of bliss, you'll be changing your tune about me."

His gaze moves over my body in a suggestive way, and my face warms under his gaze.

"Why don't you look up the real ice princess? I'm sure she'd be more than happy to fulfill her duties with you," I say with a huff, opening my bag to rummage for my keys.

Jordie's shoulders straighten. "I don't want the real ice princess. I want you."

He says it so casually that for a second, I almost believe him. But then I remember where we are, and who he is. He's not the kind of guy who'll take you out for a nice dinner and ask you questions about your childhood or what book you're reading.

He's the kind of guy who'll stick you at the end of the table in the VIP section at a club, spill his drink on you all night, and throw a hissy fit when you won't go down on him after two seconds of foreplay.

And that's what makes saying no to him so easy—and even a little fun.

"You'd better get back to your sausage fest," I say, nodding behind him as I fish for my keys inside my purse. "They'll set you up with some wide-eyed twenty-year-old, and you'll forget all about me by midnight. It'll be like none of this ever happened."

I flash Jordie a fake smile before turning on my heel to leave. Within seconds, he's in front of me again, his tall, muscular frame blocking my view of the parking lot.

I size him up. Dark, unruly hair. Blue eyes. Full, sensual lips for mouthing inflammatory things like, "Are you shedding your uterine lining?"

Seriously, who says things like that?

"Tomorrow night," he says firmly.

"I'm busy tomorrow."

"Okay, what about Sunday?" He shifts.

"I'm busy Sunday too."

"Church girl?" he asks, arching a brow.

"Something like that." I let out an exasperated sigh.

"Okay, fine, no weekend dates. What about Tuesday? No one's busy on a Tuesday."

"Don't you have practice on Tuesdays?"

"Yeah, but we're typically done by one."

"Well, I have book club."

He pauses for a moment, looking impressed. Something tells me this man doesn't date a lot of women who read.

"Wednesday then."

Jesus Christ, can't this guy take a hint?

"I volunteer on Wednesdays."

"Oh, really? Where?" His deep voice rumbles pleasantly, momentarily distracting me.

I roll my eyes. "At the animal shelter downtown."

"Me too," he says, cocking his head to the side, challenging me.

"Well, I guess I'll see you there, then," I say sarcastically, pushing past him and quickly crossing the street.

My little white sedan is waiting for me a few rows away, and I pick up the pace, silently praying that he's finally given up the fight.

"I'm looking forward to it," he calls, his voice carrying easily over the parking lot.

Sure, bud, keep telling yourself that.

• • •

The next day, I'm sitting on the floor of my apartment, shoveling herb crackers and brie into my mouth like it's my job, and trying to convince one of my best friends that a date with Jordie Prescott is a very, very bad idea.

"I think he sounds sexy," Aurora says, tossing her wavy strawberry-blond hair over her shoulder.

Downing the rest of my chardonnay and reaching for the bottle, I don't respond. It's going to take about a gallon of wine to get Aurora to lay off. Thankfully, I have a secret weapon—our other best friend, MK, the smartest, most logical person I know.

"The statistical possibility of sustaining a romantic relationship with a professional athlete is astronomically low," MK says, tucking her hair behind one ear.

"Who said anything about a relationship? Just go out with him, get a free meal, get laid, and never speak to the guy again," Aurora says with a sly grin, resting her elbows on the glass coffee table.

"He's on my dad's team. There's a good chance I *will* see him again, whether I like it or not."

Aurora frowns. "It's not like you go to games or anything."

"She's right," MK says with a nod. "Your blatant avoidance of your father's work life is notable. Especially when many people in your position would exploit the opportunity for entertainment it offers."

I glare in MK's direction, and she stares back at me matter-of-factly. "I thought you were on my side."

"I'm on the side of truth and facts," she says, beaming.

"Well, *my* truth is that I don't date—"

"Hockey players," my best friends say in unison.

"We know about your stupid rule," Aurora mutters, rolling her eyes.

"It's prudent." MK shrugs. "I support it."

"Of course you do, Mary Katherine," Aurora says with a mocking tone.

MK cringes at the use of her full name, and I shoot Aurora a warning look. When she raises her hands in surrender, I sigh loudly, holding my face in my hands.

"I never should have said yes to going to that stupid gala."

"Oh, sweetie, you were just helping your dad out. I'm sure he really appreciated it." Aurora reaches out and rubs my back with one hand, slicing me another triangle of brie with the other.

"He should have asked Faith to do it instead. She's the sweet one."

"And by Faith you mean your sister who is happily married with two children under the age of four? Right, she's the perfect candidate to be auctioned off at a charity event."

MK giggles, but all I can do is groan and try to

comfort myself with more cheese.

"Okay, enough of this. Let's talk about something other than my problems. What's up with you two? MK, whatever happened to that web developer you were talking to?" I force a smile on my face and look enthusiastically at a wide-eyed MK.

"Oh, um, Conrad? It's a funny story, actually—"

"Huh-uh, no way." Aurora cuts her off, waving a hand in the air. "I'm sorry, MK, we'll get back to Conrad in a minute. But there's no way we're letting you off the hook about this Jordie thing. He won you fair and square. You've got to deliver."

"Aurora, do you hear yourself right now? He won me? What is this, the seventeenth century?"

"Actually, the purchasing of human beings is still a problem to this day," MK says.

"That is so not the point I'm trying to make right now."

She taps at her phone, then holds it up to display an article she's pulled up on the statistics and dangers of human trafficking.

"Okay, sure, it's still a problem. And that's why I'm under no obligation to follow through on this stupid date that will end in nothing but disappointment for both of us." I lean back and rest my head on the chair behind me, exhausted by my own frustration and maybe a little tipsier than I realized.

"All I'm saying," Aurora says gently, "is don't knock it till you try it. He could surprise you."

"I've spent my entire life around hockey players. Trust me, absolutely nothing about him could possibly surprise me."

"But he's a rookie," MK says.

Confused, I turn and look at her.

"He's only been on the team one year. He's a rookie," she says again, displaying his stats and profile from the team's website on her phone.

"And your point is . . ."

"My point is that he's new to the team, and that makes him a new data set. If you go into an experiment convinced that your hypothesis is correct, your bias will skew the results. You have to be neutral."

Aurora chimes in, looking pleased. "See? Even science is on my side. You have to keep an open mind."

"Oh yeah? And have you been neutral about Conrad, Miss I Know Everything About Everything?"

"You don't have to be neutral about positive results after you've already received them," MK says, a sneaky grin spreading across her face.

"Oh my God, tell us everything!"

Aurora and I sip our wine while MK tells us about her latest nerd crush, a shy blush spreading across her chest. I'm happy for her, really, I am, but something nags at me in the back of my mind while she tells her story.

I don't care if science is against me. I don't care if they think I should give Jordie a chance. My gut makes my decisions for me, not other people, and certainly not the kinds of theories and equations normally used with algorithms and test tubes.

And right now, what my gut is telling me is crystal clear. I'm focusing on *me*, not on some twenty-five-year-old rookie hockey player.

CHAPTER FOUR

The Things We Do for Love

Jordie

It's Wednesday afternoon, and while that usually means getting stretched and massaged and ready for Friday night's game, instead I'm on my way to the animal shelter downtown.

The building is much bigger than I expected. After parking my truck in the lot, I head toward the entrance, momentarily stalling as I try to decide between the door for the adoption center or the door marked ANIMAL SHELTER. But once inside, I see that they both lead to the same place—a small front lobby with a teenage girl sitting behind the counter. It smells like a wet dog, and the sound of barking comes from somewhere deeper inside the building.

She looks up from her textbook and offers me a

slow smile. "Can I help you?"

"Yeah, I'm, um, meeting a friend of mine here to volunteer. Harper Allen. Any idea where she might be?"

The girl nods, her ponytail bobbing. "Oh, Harper's the best. She's back by the loading dock right now. She should be just about finished unloading the truckload of dog food."

I nod. "Cool. Just point me in the right direction, if you don't mind," I say, flashing her my best smile. The smile is genuine, because if Harper's almost finished, maybe it means we can get out of here and go grab a drink or something.

When I locate Harper at the far end of the warehouse, I see that she's not alone. A thirty-something guy with wire-framed glasses and a trimmed beard is standing beside her, laughing at something she's just said. I hate him immediately.

I take a few steps closer and Harper looks up, her eyes widening as she spots me.

"Jordie," she says evenly. If she's surprised to see me, she doesn't let on. "What brings you here?"

I shrug, trying to act casual. "Thought I'd lend a hand and volunteer today."

The guy next to Harper straightens like improving his posture will somehow help, even though I tower over the dude by at least six inches. "We could always use the help. Right, Harp?"

He calls her Harp? There's another thing I hate. Immensely.

When Harper moves to shift around him and the table stacked with boxes so she can face me, his hand touches her waist as she passes. A hot streak of jealousy flashes through me so suddenly that my chest tightens. *What the hell, Jordie?*

A quick glance at Harper's calm demeanor tells me she wasn't at all surprised by the slight touch. Maybe he touches her often. Maybe in other places. Maybe she likes it.

And there's that kick of jealousy again.

Fuck. Get it together, man. I don't know what it is about this girl, but something about her majorly throws me off my game. I take a slow, deep breath to compose myself.

Harper stops in front of me and offers me a tight smile. "Can I speak with you in private?"

Her eyes are the prettiest shade of brown, like warm melted chocolate.

"Sure thing." I grin back, even though I'm fairly certain she's only asked for privacy so she can tell me off out of earshot of her douchey admirer. It's something, I guess.

Harper leads the way across the warehouse, and I try my best to keep my eyes off her ass. It doesn't work out very well. Just like the other night at the auction, there's a pressure behind my zipper, even though all we've done is exchange a handful of words.

Her fiery attitude sharply contrasts with her figure, which is petite and decidedly feminine. I have no idea which I'm enjoying more—her tough exterior or that lush body.

When we have a little privacy, she spins to face me. "Cut the crap, Jordie. I know you're not here to volunteer."

"I am. I swear." And to spend a little time working side by side with her so I can start winning her over. Because, bet be dammed, my male pride is on the line here.

Harper gives me a wary look. "Okay then. You can start by cleaning the bathrooms in the adoption center. The women's toilet is clogged. Have fun."

Well, fuck. Maybe I didn't think this plan

through.

Cleaning bathrooms and unclogging toilets isn't what I had in mind for today. Laughing while we worked together, and maybe cutting out early to grab a bite to eat was what I'd envisioned. I don't even clean my own place, and now I'm doing it for the good of humanity?

But I force a smile onto my lips, because the last thing I'll do is let Harper see me quit. "With pleasure."

Harper grins back, seeming to enjoy my obvious discomfort. "Great. Well, the cleaning supplies are in the back closet"—she points—"on the shelf marked cleaning supplies."

"Self-explanatory. I like it."

She nods once and gives me a cheerful little wave before heading back toward the loading dock, where her friend is stacking boxes of pet food and yet still keeping an eye on us.

With a whispered curse, I trudge off toward the back hall that Harper indicated and find the supply closet. When I emerge with a mop, bucket, and toilet plunger, Harper's eyes widen from across the room. Maybe she thought I'd fold at her suggestion that I clean bathrooms. Clearly, she underestimated how badly I want this date.

Two hours later, I've cleaned all six urinals in the men's room, mopped the floors, and cleaned every stall in the women's restroom, including fixing the clogged toilet. Now all I want is a hot shower and a lobotomy, because I didn't think something so vile could come out of a chick.

Jesus, that was nasty. I suppress a shudder as I shove the bucket and mop back into place inside the closet.

When I see Harper waiting for me in the hall, I stop short, not expecting her to be here. And definitely not giving me a soft look.

"You actually stayed." Her tone is filled with surprise.

I nod. "Yeah, both men's and women's bathrooms are done."

She licks her lips as her gaze settles on mine. "I'm impressed."

I shrug like the last two hours were nothing. Like I wasn't about to puke up my lunch when I changed all the urinal cakes. "Just happy to do my part."

"Well, believe me, it's appreciated." She hesitates, losing some of her earlier bravado, like she doesn't know what to say.

"So you come here every Wednesday?" I ask.

She smiles. "For the last two years, yeah."

God, her mouth is perfect. "That's awfully kind of you."

She shrugs. "I usually just hang out with the puppies and play with them. My building doesn't allow dogs, and I want one, desperately. So, believe me, it's not all that altruistic."

Chuckling, I nod. "I see. Well, if you're about done, maybe we could go grab a drink or something?"

Harper shifts, her chin lifting so she can meet my eyes. "I'm sorry, Jordie, but I can't."

"I know you said you don't like hockey players, but let me prove you wrong. It's one date. What are you so afraid of?"

Footsteps approach from behind us, and then there's a deep chuckle.

"Did I just overhear you ask my daughter out?" Coach Allen stops beside Harper and gives her a one-armed hug.

My heart thuds once. *Shit*. But I recover quickly, flashing him an easy smile. "Well, yeah. I won a date with her fair and square at the auction, and she refuses to go out with me."

Coach shrugs, chuckling again like he's amused by this. "Well, I trust her judgment."

Harper grins, and then loops her arm through her dad's. "Ready for dinner?"

He nods. "I'm a little early. But I sure am."

"Cool. Let's roll. And, Jordie," she says, looking my way one last time. "Thanks for today."

• • •

"What might you have done to upset her?" Grant, our team captain, asks as we change out of our pads after practice on Thursday.

I snort. "How much time do you have?" I've just finished telling him how spectacularly Harper turned me down. *Again*. This time *after* I spent two hours cleaning toilets.

He chuckles, but it's not a mocking sound. "Just start at the beginning, big guy."

So I do, telling him about the terse exchange Harper and I had after the auction, where I might or might not have implied she had PMS, and where I also flashed a big wad of cash in order to impress her when I got her a drink.

I leave out the part where I made a bet I can get her to fall for me. Partly because she doesn't know about that, and partly because I'm a little ashamed I actually did it. Then I finish by telling him how I showed up *uninvited* to where she volunteers.

Grant clears his throat. "That all of it?"

I nod. "Basically. Am I screwed or what?"

He tilts his head, thinking it over. Grant is one of the most levelheaded, dependable guys I know. I respect the hell out of him and trust his opinion.

"That depends," he says with a sigh.

"On?"

"How badly you want to win her over."

I consider his question. Why *is* this so important to me?

Maybe it's because Harper is the first girl to turn me down in, well, forever. But it's more than that. Something about her has gotten under my skin.

She doesn't date hockey players, and she's extremely vocal about that. She's my coach's daughter, for fuck's sake, which means she's completely off-limits. I shouldn't want her, because on paper she's all wrong for me, but of course all of this just makes me want her so much more.

Admittedly, I don't know a lot about women. Yeah, I know how to make sure they have fun in bed, but that takes patience, not skill. I'm no quitter, so satisfaction is guaranteed. And while I may not know a ton about women, I know I like Harper. I like her in a way that I can't explain, which is confusing as fuck. And let's not forget that she's fucking gorgeous.

"That bad, huh?" he says at my speechlessness.

I grin, trying to lighten the mood. "Yeah, I guess I've got it pretty bad."

Grant considers this, watching me. "You've never had a serious girlfriend, have you?"

I give my head a shake.

Basically, I'm the human equivalent of a spork. I serve a purpose, filling a temporary void, and then people move on, upgrading to the thing they wanted most all along. Harper refusing to go on a date with me is bringing up my abandonment issues— my sister the therapist's term, not mine. And even if I don't like to admit it, yeah, I'm pretty much a textbook case for abandonment issues.

The truth is that no one has ever really loved me. Not really. No one was ever there for me when I needed them. Dad died when I was thirteen, which was hard. It was awful. But worse was feeling like I lost my mom too. Even though she was still there, she also wasn't, because she threw herself into so many other things, saying she was *finding herself*. Mom was a free spirit, and when pursuing her hobbies and passions became her life's focus, my sister and I were pushed aside.

On the day of the NHL draft, one of the biggest events of my life, she was on a spiritual retreat in Arizona. The night of my first ever pro game, she was on a flight to Australia for a course to become an accredited guru. And while other guys' families are blowing up their phones after a game with congratulations, mine's always silent. It hurts, a hell of a lot, but I keep it pretty well locked down.

"Why now? Why her?" Grant asks.

"I don't know, all right? I just want my shot." Groaning, I say, "Tell me what to do."

"Not everyone's gonna like you, Jordie."

It's the same speech my older sister gave me

when I couldn't get along with the playground bullies in middle school. I didn't like hearing it then, and I like it even less now.

"Yeah, but this girl? I need her to, okay?" There's an edge of desperation to my voice that even I don't recognize.

Grant nods, seeming to read something in my expression. "Then don't give up on her. Fight like hell to get her attention, and when you do, make sure you keep it by giving her the real Jordan Prescott, not the guy she thinks you are."

I release a slow sigh. It's not bad advice.

I think about his relationship with Ana. It's something to envy, for sure, but I know it wasn't always easy. I was there during those first few rocky months. When she found out she was pregnant, I remember how scared he was. How uncertain it all felt.

And look how they turned out. Holy power couple.

"Nice work out there today," Coach Allen says, stopping beside us in the locker room.

"Thanks, Coach," Grant says, shoving his feet into sneakers.

I stand up and pull a sweatshirt on over my head, then grab my bag.

Coach looks up from his iPad and meets my eyes. "How's it going with Harper?"

I shift, securing the bag over one shoulder. "It's not. She shot me down."

Coach shakes his head, a smirk tugging on his lips. "She's always been a stubborn girl. Spirited, her mother liked to say."

Harper's playing hard to get, so maybe it's time to try a new angle. Feeling bold, I smile at him. "You wouldn't, by any chance, give me her number, would you?"

Coach Allen laughs, a deep sound that gives me the impression he's not the least bit annoyed by my infatuation with his daughter. But, hey, we're all adults, here, right?

"Oh, what the hell," Coach says, still chuckling. "You've got some balls, kid. I'll give you that." He jots down the digits on a piece of scrap paper and then hands it to me. "You're a good kid. Don't prove me wrong."

"Yes, sir." I nod solemnly, unable to wipe the smile from my face.

"You are so fucked," Grant mutters under his breath when Coach Allen leaves.

Don't I know it.

CHAPTER FIVE

Catch and Release

Harper

My phone buzzes, and I pry my attention away from the article I've been working on about Snapchat filters just long enough to see that it's a text. Anyone I work with knows it's easier to reach me through our internal chat system, and my friends know better than to text me on a writing-from-home day.

For a second, my brain goes to the worst. What if something happened to Dad? What if this is a stranger letting me know that he's unconscious somewhere and waiting for an ambulance?

But that's crazy, right? If something happened to my dad, I'd get a call. What kind of monster would send a text letting you know your father had a heart attack?

Surprised by my ability to freak myself out, I tap the screen and open the notification, my brows scrunching together in disbelief as I read the text.

Hey, it's Jordie. I don't know about you, but I'm still in need of some major rehab after volunteering the other day. Let's eat our body weight in tapas and finally admit how we feel about each other.

Stunned, I stare at the screen. *You've got to be freaking kidding me.*

My fingers fly furiously over the digital keyboard, my response quick and to the point.

How did you get this number???

Three little dots instantly appear on his side of the screen.

Snapchat filters are the last thing on my mind now. The only thing left is pure, unadulterated frustration. Can't this guy take a hint? Did the first five times I said *no* mean nothing? And, seriously, how *did* he get my number?

Your dad decided to take a chance

on me. Why won't you?

I drop my phone on my desk and rake my fingers through my hair. My own father is responsible for this? Suddenly, I find myself half wishing someone would call me with the news that he's been found unconscious somewhere.

Not that I should be surprised. Dad just wants me to be happy, and he doesn't know about my no-players rule. It would be too difficult to explain to him without simultaneously hurting his feelings. Damn, I hate it when I can't stay mad at him.

I'm working. Sorry, can't text.

It's a white lie, but hopefully a convincing one. I haven't worked somewhere that controlling since high school, but Jordie doesn't know that. For all he knows, I'm flipping burgers at a greasy spoon around the corner while my boss watches over my shoulder.

To my horror, my phone buzzes again, but instead of two short, consecutive bursts, it keeps buzzing. It's ringing. He's calling me. Seriously, will this guy not take a hint?

I clear my throat before swiping to answer the call, cautiously holding the phone to my ear, like he'll find some way to jump through it. "You're ridiculous, you know that?"

"I think *dedicated* is the word you're looking for." His voice is deep, and it rumbles pleasantly through the line. But just because he has a nice voice doesn't mean I'm going to go out with him.

"You're quickly becoming the textbook definition of insane," I fire back.

"Oh, come on. Since when are we supposed to deny the laws of attraction?"

I smile and shake my head. "Why do you want to go out with me so bad?"

It's an honest question. Jordie is a professional athlete. He's young, he's gorgeous, and judging from how forward he's been with me, he's used to getting what he wants. He could just as easily turn up at the stadium bar after practice and find a gaggle of drooling groupies to take home. There's no reason for him to keep striking out with me.

"Because I like you." He says it matter-of-factly, like he's explaining the ingredients of a PB and J.

"You don't even know me."

"I know you volunteer at the local animal shelter."

"That doesn't count. I told you that."

"Doesn't mean it's not something I like about you."

Fine. I'll take the bait. "What else do you like about me?"

He chuckles, and I can practically hear his smile grow wider through the phone. "I like that you're honest and speak your mind. Even if you decide to shut me down."

"You mean *when* I shut you down."

"See …I also like that you're confident. And stubborn as hell."

"Hey!" Despite myself, I can't keep from laughing.

"I'm trying to take a page out of your honesty book. Oh, that too. Books. I like that you read."

I raise one eyebrow. "Literacy seems like a low bar for attraction."

"You know what I mean. The book club."

"How do you know about book club?"

"You told me. The first night we met."

"Oh, right. How could I forget the first night you stalked me?"

We both laugh, and for a second, this whole thing feels natural. Jordie's easy to talk to, and he's clearly into me. Maybe I was wrong to rule out *all* hockey players. Maybe MK was right. Hell, maybe I should give the new data set a chance.

There are a lot of things to like about Jordie. His big, hard body is an obvious one. His persistence. His dedication. His infatuation with me is another obvious front-runner. There's something in his eyes too. And my dad trusts him, apparently, since he's the one who gave Jordie my number.

"Come on, Harper. One night. That's all I'm asking for."

I pause, twisting the end of my hair around my finger. "I mean, I guess—"

"Yeah, no, I'll be there in a sec," Jordie says distractedly, cutting me off mid-sentence.

"What?"

"Hey, sorry, I just got called back for some power-play drills. You know how it is. The team comes first, blah, blah, blah."

And there it is. The reminder I needed of why this would never work between us.

I straighten my shoulders. "That's fine. I've got to go anyway."

His rich, deep chuckle washes over me. "You're going to leave me without an answer?"

"I've already given you my answer. Several times."

"Well, you have my number now. Feel free to use it."

I roll my eyes. And to think I was *this* close to letting this guy take me out.

• • •

A few hours later, I've wrapped up the article I was writing, touched up my makeup, and headed out to my favorite coffee shop for book club with the girls. Currently, I'm sitting in a plush, dark blue armchair listening to MK and Aurora argue about our latest read. But by the looks of it, my best friends are probably regretting sharing a loveseat right about now.

I take a long sip of my coffee while the girls continue to argue. One of them thinks the heroine in the book is making a huge mistake agreeing to be a submissive for the growly hero. The other thinks it's romantic and steamy, and the whole point of the book. It doesn't take a genius to figure out which one is which.

"She's being an absolute idiot," MK says, throwing her hands in the air.

"They're in *love*," Aurora snaps.

"Fine. They're *idiots* in love."

"What do you expect her to do, not give in to temptation and be bored and miserable for the rest of her life?"

"He's a control freak. It'll never work. And they're foolish to pretend they're equipped for any kind of commitment."

"Harps, back me up on this. True love conquers all, right?" Aurora gives me a desperate look while MK shoots me eye-daggers.

"Actually, I was hoping to discuss Annabelle's monologue about pursuing a future for herself, and not letting her father's expectations dictate her actions," I say, flipping through my book to find the underlined passage.

When I look up, MK and Aurora are staring

blankly at me.

"Am I the only one who wanted to discuss the monologue?"

"I worry about you sometimes," Aurora murmurs, tucking her long locks behind her ear.

"Even I was able to deduce that the forbidden romance is the preferred topic of book club discussion," MK says.

I don't respond, simply shrug and wave my hand for them to resume. They pick right back up in the middle of their argument, and I start to tune them out.

It's always the same debate. Is love worth the sacrifice, whether that sacrifice is as small as cutting your hair or as monumental as abandoning a stable, albeit boring life for an adventure on the wild side? My friends have strong opinions on either end of the spectrum, but I often find myself vacillating somewhere in between.

I guess I haven't experienced the sweeping romance I read about on the pages of my favorite novels. Haven't had my heart broken so badly that I cried myself to sleep at night. Sure, I've had a handful of relationships, and some have ended up being disastrous, but I'm not quite as solid in my beliefs when it comes to love.

For as confident as I am in all other areas of my life, I second-guess myself with those things, which is why some hard-and-fast rules can really come in handy. Like my one about not dating hockey players. I also have very strict rules about open-mouth chewers and nail-biters. No thank you on both counts.

"Hello, earth to Harper? There's a hottie at twelve o'clock who won't stop making eyes at the back of your head." Aurora's voice snaps me out of my own inner monologue.

I follow her gaze to check out who she's talking about, and when I see the subject in question, my heart skips a beat for the second time today. Only this time, it's one hundred percent warranted. Because suddenly, I'm not just here at a coffee shop having book club with my friends. *Oh no.* This situation just got a whole lot weirder.

"That's Jordie," I say, and my friends let out tiny gasps, their mouths falling open.

It's Aurora who finds her voice first. "What the hell, Harper? You didn't tell us he was a freaking twelve out of ten."

"Maybe if we just ignore him, he'll go away," I

mutter under my breath.

"Why on earth would we want him to do that?" she asks, sounding offended.

"Be realistic, Harper. Even from an outsider's perspective, he is very attractive. Genetically pleasing, some might even say," MK says with a smile.

"That boy is next-level hot, and even MK wants to make babies with him," Aurora adds with authority.

My gaze darts over to MK, who's surely about to dispute this. *Right?*

But no, she's grinning like a loon and lets out a short laugh. "I said what I said."

I huff out a sigh and contemplate stabbing him with my coffee stir stick. Actually, my first plan might be better—ignore him and see if he goes away.

CHAPTER SIX

Female Empowerment

Jordie

"Nice shirt, Jordie. Pink really suits you," Teddy says with a chuckle when I slide into my chair at the coffee shop.

"It's salmon," I say, looking down at the button-down shirt I'm wearing, which is, well, *pink*. It was a stupid idea. It was supposed to make me look less imposing. Less like a testosterone-fueled jock. More sensitive. I'm not sure it's working.

Teddy squints at me. "What . . . *are you drunk?*"

"No, fucker," I mutter.

The rest of the guys filter in, and once we're all seated at the little round table with coffees in front of us, I shove a copy of the book I brought at Teddy. "Here. Take this."

"What's this?" With a skeptical look, he turns it over and inspects the back cover. "Did you just hand me a romance novel?" His mouth quirks up in amusement.

"It's our book club read." I grin, nodding.

"For fuck's sake, Jordie. You worry me. You really do."

A few of my teammates agreed to meet me at the coffee shop tonight, and it cost me a pretty penny. But, hey, at least they're here.

"You should really read that, dude," Asher says with a smirk, shoving it closer to Teddy. "Maybe you can finally figure out how to satisfy your woman in the bedroom."

"Fuck off," Teddy says with a scowl.

Justin tugs his baseball cap lower, frowning at me. There aren't many people here at the coffee shop at eight o'clock on a weeknight, but I'm sure he's still hoping he doesn't get recognized. As the team's starting center, Justin Brady draws a lot of attention wherever he goes.

"I don't care that you're paying me fifty bucks to be here . . . this is the stupidest idea you've ever had to win a bet."

"Wait a second, you're only getting fifty? He gave me a hundred." Asher leans back, crossing his bulky arms over his chest with a pleased expression.

"You guys are getting *paid?*" Teddy groans. "What the actual fuck, Jordie?"

"It's not about the bet, okay," I say in a hushed voice, pulling my chair closer to our table. "And sorry, TK."

Teddy flips me the middle finger.

"Fine. Then let me rephrase that. It's the most pathetic way to get pussy I've ever seen," Justin says with an eye roll.

"Yeah. Surely there are plenty of other women you could stick your dick into. Why does it have to be this one?" Asher asks, tipping his chin to where she sits across the room.

I sneak another look at Harper and feel like I've been sucker-punched. She's wearing a pair of black leggings and an army-green button-down shirt. Her legs are crisscrossed under her and her hair is in loose waves over her shoulder, but I can't see her face from this angle.

Justin leans forward, his dark eyes on mine.

"And don't say it's not the bet again. I know you, dude, you're competitive. You want to win."

God, I hate how well they know me. I also wish I'd never made that idiotic bet. A bet that if I lose, I'll *never* hear the end of.

"Well, maybe it's a little bit about the bet," I say in a low voice. "But, dude, look at her. I want my shot, all right?"

I glance across the room to where Harper is seated with her girlfriends. She hasn't spotted me yet, which means she's completely in her element—not trying to impress anyone or censor herself. Her friend says something that makes her laugh, and Harper tosses her head back with a chuckle, then stuffs a huge piece of orange-cranberry scone in her mouth.

Damn, that looks good. I should've gotten one of those.

I drag my gaze away, realizing the guys are still waiting for my answer. "Look, she's gorgeous. Funny. Smart. I want to go out with her, okay? Is that so hard to understand?"

All of that is true. But it's more than that. Maybe because I find the whole *no, Jordie, I don't want your cock* act fucking adorable. It doesn't happen often, and what can I say? I'm a sucker for the chase.

Justin lets out a defeated sigh under his breath. "I hope you know what you're doing, rookie."

I hope so too. Considering her dad has control over me playing the sport I love for a living.

"I think it's time we have the talk with the rookie," Asher says, grinning like a fool.

Boy, this should be good. "And what talk would that be?"

"The birds and the bees."

I roll my eyes. "Fuck off, Ashe."

He smirks. "There are more than those special moments you share with your fist, Jordie. I just want you to be prepared."

"I'm good, thanks."

I zone out while he and TK ramble on, some idiotic advice about when you're going down on a woman, to start off like you're a butterfly sipping nectar, and to finish like you're a Rottweiler devouring a steak.

It's honestly not bad advice, but I'd never tell them that.

"So, have you actually read the book, or what are we doing here?" Asher asks, halfheartedly flipping through the pages of the copy in front of him. "Oh, I know. We can read the dirty parts." His lips curve up in a grin.

"Relax, dude. We're not here to talk about the book. Just be my wingmen."

Asher shrugs. "Fine. You don't have to be a dick about it."

"Bro, I think we've been spotted," Justin says under his breath, staring across the room.

"Be cool, guys." Asher coughs the words into his fist. "Be cool.

I see a flash of movement in my peripheral vision, but I don't dare look up. Not yet.

"Jordie?" Harper stops beside our table, gazing down at me with a quizzical expression. Her brown eyes are narrowed on mine, and her mouth presses into a firm line.

"Oh. Hey, Harper." My *I'm as surprised as you are* tone is on-fucking-point. Mentally patting myself on the back, I straighten and flash her a smile. "What are you doing here?"

Her mouth opens, and when her gaze darts to

her friends, the dark-haired one flashes Harper an encouraging thumbs-up. A good sign, but I work to keep my face neutral, because it's way too early to celebrate this as a victory. For all I know, she's about to file a restraining order, or worse, kick me in the balls.

"Just having a book club meeting." Her voice is curt, unamused, like she's bored with me and this entire conversation.

We'll change that, sweetheart.

I scoff, loudly, probably overselling the coincidence. "Weird. Me too."

She exhales, glancing down at the paperback copy of *Destined for Him*, complete with a man-chest cover, on the table in front of me. "Interesting. It's the same book my friends and I are discussing."

"Man, the things we have in common . . . they just keep piling up. Am I right?"

She blinks at me, her lips parted.

"Hey. Harper, right?" Asher gives her a cocky grin.

She gives him a polite smile and a little wave. "Hello."

"Well, great talk, guys. Now get lost," I grumble.

"Have some manners, dude," Justin mutters under his breath.

With a few more eye rolls, they get up and push in their chairs.

Teddy pauses, lingering by the table. "Hey, Jordie, how about that fifty bucks you owe me?"

I reach into my pocket and shove a fifty at him. "Here you go. Now beat it."

With a chuckle, Teddy joins the others, and they take off toward the door. So far, tonight's cost me two hundred dollars, and I didn't even get one of those scones.

"Do you want to sit down? Maybe share something from the pastry counter?" I ask, looking up at her.

Harper lowers herself into the chair Asher just vacated. "What are you really doing here? I refuse to believe you're actually reading this." She picks up my copy of the book.

"Of course I am."

"Right," she says dryly. After glancing back at

her friends, she meets my eyes again, this time with a challenging expression. "So, what were your thoughts on the submission theme in the opening scene?"

I lick my lips, kind of loving the fact that we're actually going to talk about the book. I bought it on a lark after seeing it inside her bag at the animal shelter. Then I found out from her dad which coffee shop she had her book club at. Stalker-ish? Yeah, maybe a little. But I like to think of it as determination.

"I loved that, actually," I say, clearing my throat. "And just so we're clear, it's a no on the pastries?"

"Stop stalling, Jordie. I know you didn't read it."

"For your information, I loved the beginning. The part where Sebastian says to Annabelle that she's his whole world and that he'd rather die than see her hurt?" I touch my chest. "That hit me straight in the feels."

She smiles, softening the slightest bit. "I liked that part too. What about the scene with the blindfold?"

Gathering momentum, I lean forward. "So

fucking hot." *As was the thing I did to myself in the shower directly after reading that scene.* "The amount of trust needed between two people when blindfolds and toys come into play? It was . . . *educational.* I'd never thought about that before."

She nods, her mouth lifting in a smile. "I know, right?"

"It's a very boundary-pushing book."

She nods again.

Honestly, reading the book was pretty eye-opening. The paragraphs filled with descriptions of deep longing and heart-aching love made something knot in my stomach. I've had my fair share of dates and enjoyed the company of many women, but I've never actually experienced anything remotely like the soul-touching deep connections the book described.

Hell, I've never experienced anything deeper than a few fleeting moments of pleasure. A couple of fun-filled nights, or maybe even a few weeks, but when it ended, I was never upset. Never felt like half of me was missing, or that there was a hole in my heart. Which makes me wonder why I've never been in love.

Then again, maybe everything described on

these pages is total bullshit.

But even as I try to console myself with that, I know it's a lie. I've watched many of my teammates fall deeply in love and settle down. I've overheard their cheesy phone calls with their significant others while we were traveling. It sure didn't seem like any of them were faking it.

Harper's mouth twitches. "What did you think about the part when the alien came in and abducted her?"

My stomach knots. *Shit.* I have no idea what she's talking about. "Oh, absolutely insane. I couldn't believe that happened."

She scoffs. "See? I knew you didn't read it. You are so full of shit."

I hold up both hands. "Okay, you busted me. But I *am* reading it. I'm only at page . . ." I flip to the dog-eared page I left off on last night after my spank session. "Fifty-six."

She softens somewhat, her lips parting.

"I wouldn't lie to you, Harper. I really am reading it. And it's a good read so far."

Before she has the chance to reply, her friends get up and approach us. They stop beside our table and look at us with knowing smiles.

"Hey, Harper, we're going to take off. Enjoy your date," one of her friends says, setting Harper's purse on the table in front of her.

"It's not a *date*," she says, her voice strained.

"Are you going to introduce me to your friends?" I ask.

"Nope," she says. "'Bye, guys."

One of her friends rolls her eyes at Harper, and the other gives me a smile. Harper's definitely told them about me. It's something, I guess.

"I'm Aurora," the redhead says, holding out her hand toward me.

"Jordan Prescott." I return her handshake with a short, efficient pump.

"MK," the other girl says, a soft blush on her cheeks.

"Hello." I grin at her.

"Well, text us later," Aurora says with a big *you're in so much trouble* grin at Harper.

I chuckle into my fist while Harper shoots them daggers with her eyes.

"So, did you finish?" I ask, drawing her attention back to me.

"Hmm?" She tucks her hair behind one ear.

"The book. You read the whole thing?"

She nods, crossing one leg over the other. "Twice."

"Wow. Impressive."

"Not really. It's more just a testament to my lack of a social life," she says, and I grin at her honesty. "What's been your favorite part so far?" she asks, her eyes dancing on mine.

I consider her question. It's not an easy one to answer. Mostly, I liked the sex scene, but I don't think that answer will earn me any brownie points with her. *Dig deeper, Jordie.*

"I guess I liked how he, I mean, Sebastian, had to be . . ." I search for the right word, snapping my fingers when I find it. ". . . vulnerable with her. He had to be strong, but also honest and raw, and just, um . . . like emotionally connected to her on a deeper level that wasn't just about sex. I liked that, I guess."

For a second, I worry I've said too much, revealed too much of myself and my desperate desire to connect with someone on a level that's about more than just swapping a couple of orgasms.

But Harper's eyes stay locked on mine, and she chews her lower lip thoughtfully. "*Hmm.*"

"What about you? What's your favorite thing about it, Miss I'm Such an Overachiever, I Read it Twice." I grin at her.

She smiles up at me, and damn, my knees feel a little weak. She's beautiful when she smiles. "I guess the female empowerment angle. I love that about romance novels. They're books written *by* women, *for* women, for the sole purpose of illustrating that women deserve pleasure and love. Throughout history, that certainly hasn't always been the case. Women have been persecuted and made to feel less than for centuries. In romance, it's the opposite."

"Wow. I never thought about that. That's cool." Especially the pleasure part—because, *hello*, I'd accept a starting role as her Fabio any day.

Harper straightens the book on the table, nodding. "In school, all the assigned reading was about boys, men . . . off doing things. Sometimes they were about women, but—and feel free to call me pessimistic here—they weren't exactly empowering or uplifting. Romance is a genre where a woman's pleasure is the entire point of the book."

"Hear, hear." I raise my coffee mug in a toast to her.

She chuckles. "Believe me, I know it's fiction, but it's also a safe place where readers trust that a woman's sexuality will be treated positively. And, I mean, that's important, isn't it?"

"Very," I choke out. She's on a roll, and there's no way I'm stopping her now.

We talk for a little while longer, and to my surprise, Harper doesn't ask any questions about the team. It's a refreshing change. Usually when I meet someone new, the first thing they do is shoot off rapid-fire questions about hockey, like that's the only topic I'm capable of talking about. Harper doesn't do that. And I like it. A lot.

After a few more minutes of conversation, Harper checks the time on her phone. "It's getting late. I'd better get going."

Swallowing my disappointment, I rise along with her. We walk to the door together, and my stomach flutters with the same feeling as when I've got the puck and we're down by one with under a minute in regulation. I've got to take my shot.

"Can I drive you home?" I ask.

"I'm parked right there." She presses a button on her key fob, and the lights flash twice on a little white sedan.

We pause on the sidewalk, and Harper turns to face me. She's so small—barely coming up to my chin, and her tits are so nice and perky. And, God, I want to kiss the fuck out of her soft mouth. Instead, I pull a deep breath into my lungs and shove one hand in my pocket.

I don't miss the way Harper's gaze tracks down my torso, briefly settling at my belt before darting away again. Maybe she's not as immune to me as she lets on.

"So, now that you know we enjoy the same reading material, will you go out with me?"

Her mouth softens. "That depends. Are you going to keep stalking me?"

My lips twitch with a smirk. "Until you say yes? Absolutely."

She laughs, shaking her head. "We'll see then."

I shrug one shoulder before holding out my hand toward her. "Okay. Well, it was nice running into you again."

She scoffs, shaking her head before gently shaking my hand. "Why do I get the feeling this won't be the last time we just happen to run into each other?"

"Persistence, Harper. It's a good thing."

Laughing, she adjusts the strap of her purse on her shoulder. "Good night, Jordie."

"Good night. Be safe."

I stand there on the sidewalk until she's safely tucked inside her car. As I watch her fasten her seat belt and pull away, an unsettled feeling washes over me.

In the past, women have entertained me in my free time, made me laugh, and yeah, even turned me on. But Harper freaking Allen laughing at my obvious discomfort? Harper . . . doing something so simple as sparring with me over a book? It has me basically losing my shit.

She's so far out of my league, it isn't even funny, but there's only one thing to do when you miss.

Take another shot.

CHAPTER SEVEN

The Best Laid Plans

Harper

I'm not sure there's anything better than driving home after a long, stressful day of work. Unless that thing is getting home, changing into sweatpants, taking off your bra, and popping open a bottle of your favorite pinot noir.

Okay, so maybe the driving home isn't the best part, but after the day I've had? I'm feeling pretty optimistic about the night ahead.

I'm lucky because I have the kind of job that allows me to work from home every once in a while. But that means that when I do go into the office, it's that much harder to sit through the hours of supervised internet browsing and meetings that really should just be emails. Those forty-five minutes we spent arguing over office refrigerator etiquette are forty-five minutes I can never get back.

At least I've got that pinot noir waiting for me at home.

The light I've been sitting at for what feels like ten minutes finally turns green, and when I press on the gas, the car lurches a little before accelerating normally. It's a little weird, but at least we're moving.

Suddenly, the car lurches again and slows down, even though my foot is still on the gas pedal. The car behind me honks loudly, and panic begins to set in. *Shit.* I turn the wheel, praying that my car will keep moving long enough to get me over to the side of the road, and to my relief, it inches out of the lane before finally sputtering to a stop.

Great. And I thought my day was starting to turn around.

Parked safely out of the way of passing traffic, I press the contact info for my dad. After the line rings for a minute or so, a familiar voice-mail message plays. "Hey, you've reached Mark Allen. Sorry I missed your call. I'm probably on the ice. Go, Hawks!"

Silently cursing the game of hockey more vehemently than I ever have before in my life, I try

Aurora, then MK, then Faith, but even my own sister doesn't pick up. Doesn't anyone answer their phone anymore?

Desperate, and starting to wonder if I'd be better off just calling a repair shop and paying the exorbitant fee for roadside service, I dial the one number I never wanted to use.

The phone rings, and within seconds, the call connects.

"So, are you finally ready to go out with me?" Jordie's voice is smooth and self-assured, and I can just imagine the satisfied look on his face.

Swallowing a heavy sigh, I force a smile instead. Even if he can't see it, I'm hoping it will make my voice sound less hostile. I really do need his help.

"Hey, uh, not exactly. My car broke down."

"Oh shit, are you okay?" He drops the cocky act, and his voice is suddenly serious and concerned. It's a little sweet, actually.

"Um, yeah. I was able to pull over before it totally died. But I'm kind of stranded right now."

"Drop a pin with your location. I'll be there as soon as I can."

He hangs up before I can respond, and within seconds, I have a new text from him.

Just send me your location and
                    hang tight.

I didn't think I was into the *knight in shining armor* type, but this whole *hero who's about to come swooping in to save the day* thing Jordie's got going on? I'm more into it than I'd like to admit.

I send him my location and lean my head on the headrest, easing out a long sigh. This hunk of metal was supposed to be my baby, the one thing I could rely on. I can't believe it's let me down already.

Ten minutes later, Jordie pulls up behind me in a large black pickup. I'd pegged him as a flashy sports car kind of guy, but this makes sense for him too.

I climb out of my car at the same time he gets out of the truck, and once again, I'm riveted by his broad frame. In well-fitting jeans and a T-shirt that perfectly showcases his firm, defined muscles, he still finds a way to look hotter than I'd like, even when rescuing a damsel in distress on the side of the road.

"Hey, Harper, are you okay?"

"Yeah, I'm fine," I mutter, running a hand self-consciously through my hair. "Can't say the same for my baby, though." I give one of my tires a little kick, squinting up at him.

Jordie grins, his gaze dropping to my mouth.

I take a moment to study him, since he's clearly looking at me. His hair is neatly trimmed on the sides and longer on top with enough messiness that I could slide my fingers right into the thick, dark strands without worry. He's young and well-built, and bursting with virile masculinity and so much confidence that it's hard to ignore. His jaw is chiseled and dusted with stubble, his cheekbones are high, and his lips are full and soft. The kind of lips that are wasted on a man.

Although, I'll bet he's a phenomenal kisser with that mouth—not that I'll ever find out. If I want Jordie to believe I'm serious about my no-hockey-players rule, I need to stand my ground. I can already tell he's the kind of guy you give an inch to, and he'll take a whole mile. And before I know what's happened, I'll be in his bed with my ankles on his shoulders while he plows away.

A hot shiver runs through me, and I shake off the mental image. *Bad Harper. He's here to help you out of a jam, not for you to ogle like some piece of meat.*

But the way those wide shoulders pull at the seam of his T-shirt is hard not to notice, and I have to force my gaze away. I refuse to stare and drool over him like some puck bunny in heat.

It's a term I've never uttered out loud before because, well, it seems a little judgmental to name-call a woman simply because she enjoys the company of a certain type of man. But something about the thought of Jordie with a bouncing blonde with stars in her eyes, willing to go home with him simply *because*, sets off a sinking feeling inside my stomach.

He's a professional athlete, not a messiah, and I won't be dropping to my knees to worship him. Although *that* mental image conjures up a strange tingling low in my stomach that I have to fight to ignore.

God, Harper. Seriously. Get your head on straight.

"What happened?" Jordie asks, thankfully interrupting my inspection of him.

I explain the various noises and lurches my car made before dying, and he nods along, his gaze fixed on mine with an intensity that sends a tingle through my core.

"Sounds like a battery issue. Or maybe the belt. Anyway, my man Miguel will figure it out. He's on his way right now."

"What? No, that's really not necessary."

"Do you know another mechanic who won't overcharge and will get you your wheels back in two days?"

Jordie flashes me that undeniable smile, and all I can do is shrug and turn away.

"Don't we need to call a tow?"

"Nope. Miguel's got it covered."

"In that case, I should call an Uber or something."

"Uh, hello, you've got an Uber right here who won't charge a dime."

I raise my eyebrows. "I know all about your stalker tendencies, Prescott. I can't trust you with the knowledge of where I live."

He laughs. "Fair enough. How about dinner then? You've got to be starving."

As if on cue, my stomach growls, and Jordie

gives me a knowing look.

"Only if I get to choose where we eat," I say.

"Fine by me. You do know this doesn't count as a date, though, right?" Jordie asks with a half smile.

"Uh, we're going to have dinner. At a restaurant. At night. Yes, this counts as a date."

"No way." He shakes his head. "This might be *a* date, but it's not *the* date I'm owed from the charity auction."

"If I go to dinner with you tonight, I'm off the hook, buddy." I plant one hand on my hip.

He crosses his muscular forearms over his bulky chest, his eyes dancing with amusement. "Come to my place then. I was planning to make spaghetti tonight anyway. Let me cook for you."

My eyes widening, I make a sound of surprise. "You cook?"

"It's spaghetti, not rocket science."

The tow truck pulls up in front of my car, and Jordie walks over to greet Miguel and sort things out. Part of me wants to put up a little fight, but I'd be lying if I said it wasn't nice to have someone take care of me, just this once.

When they reach an agreement, Miguel hands me a card and says he'll call when he has any news. Jordie helps him connect the cables, and within minutes, my car is being carried away, and it's just me, Jordie, and his truck.

"Shall we?"

He ushers me to the passenger side, holding the door open and giving me hand as I hoist myself up into the seat.

"For a non-date, you're being pretty chivalrous," I say when he settles into the driver's side next to me.

"Date or not, I know how to treat a lady."

When we get to his place, I don't know whether to be shocked or envious. Of course Jordie lives downtown in a condo with high ceilings and a killer view of the water. Of course his place is sleek and modern, and way more tastefully decorated than I anticipated.

He must have hired someone to help him. There's no way this rookie had time to shop for the perfect floor lamp to complement his plush gray sofa. Hell, I barely had time to decorate my place beyond matching my hand towels to my shower curtain. And here this guy has the perfect finishing touches, like hand-carved wooden coasters, and framed modern artwork hanging on his walls.

Although, why am I surprised, considering his exorbitant salary? *Ugh. Hockey players are so spoiled.* Actually, that's not true. I've seen first-hand how dedicated they are to their craft, how much they put their bodies through, how horrific the injuries can be when things go wrong.

"Red or white?"

Jordie interrupts my thoughts to lead me through the living room to the kitchen, which is even more beautiful, with its clean, polished stain-less-steel appliances, and a stunning black granite countertop with a pot rack hanging over it.

I have to consciously keep my mouth from fall-ing open at the sight of it all.

His place is a far cry from the smelly, shabby bachelor pad I was expecting. This is somewhere an adult who knows who they are and what's im-portant to them lives. And that's the last thing I ex-pected from Jordie.

I clear my throat and try to regain my compo-sure. "Any chance you've got a cab open?"

Jordie smiles and furrows his brow. "You're a guest in my home. I'm serving you a fresh bottle."

He pulls a bottle from the wine rack and places two glasses on the counter. After he pours, he hands one to me, and we clink glasses before taking a drink.

Damn, even his wine is better than I expected.

Okay calm down, Harper. The guy is attractive, and he has good taste. There's no need to hand over my panties, and certainly not my heart.

"Anything I can do to help with dinner?" I ask politely, watching him take a large silver pot down from the rack and fill it with water.

"All I need you to do is make yourself comfortable. And answer some of my burning questions."

Oh boy, here we go. "How about one burning question," I say cautiously, perching myself on one of the leather stools at the counter.

"Fair enough. What's with the whole *no dating hockey players* thing?"

I should have known he'd ask that. "You mean, why won't I date you?"

He shrugs, dicing a tomato with surprising precision. "I'm genuinely curious. You're an intelligent, reasonable woman. Something had to have happened for you to make a rule like that."

I sigh and take another sip of wine. "It's a long story."

"We've got all the time in the world."

"Well, let's just say that growing up with a coach for a dad is . . . tricky. We moved around a lot when I was growing up, and it was hard to make friends. Or to keep them. We didn't have a whole lot of stability. Don't get me wrong, money was never an issue, and Dad did his best. But after my mom walked out . . ."

Shit. I wasn't exactly planning on whipping out my little sob story so soon. Or ever, really.

"I didn't know about that. That must have been tough," Jordie says.

Dad's schedule wasn't just hard on us kids, it was hard on their marriage, and I had a front-row seat to the show. But I don't want to get into all of that right now.

I let out a slow breath. "It turned out okay in the end. Dad worked hard to take care of us. That just meant putting his job—and the team—first. All.

The. Time. We were always trailing along with him to practices and games and tape reviews, and we constantly had players over at our house. I know he was just doing his best to keep food on the table and give us whatever we wanted, but at the end of the day, what I really wanted was for him to be just my dad, and not someone else's coach."

It all comes out so quickly, I barely even think about it. When I look up, Jordie is looking at me with sympathy in his eyes, and I feel a pang of guilt in my chest.

"Please don't tell my dad I said that. It would break his heart."

Jordie shakes his head. "I would never. I appreciate you sharing that with me."

His blue eyes lock on mine, and that same tingle I felt earlier jolts again through my core.

"You didn't answer my question, though," he says, his tone playful.

I smile. "I'm putting myself first now. My goals, my dreams, my aspirations are my priority. And in my experience, hockey players only care about two things—their team and themselves."

He shakes his head. "That's not always true."

"Plus, they're smelly. And cocky. And rough."

"What's wrong with being rough?" he asks, his gaze briefly moving from my eyes to my lips.

And there goes that jolt—this time between my thighs.

Still, I roll my eyes.

Jordie laughs, stirring the sauce he put together while I was talking. It smells so good, my stomach growls again.

He cocks an eyebrow at me. "Food's almost done."

"I didn't say anything," I say innocently.

"You didn't have to."

He makes the final touches to our meal, and soon we're seated at his dining table, drinking and laughing and eating the delicious food I'm still shocked he knows how to make.

"Okay, fess up," I say between bites. "Where'd you learn how to cook?"

"My mom," he replies with a smile that brings crinkles to the sides of his eyes.

Something flutters in my stomach at the thought

of his mom doing that for him.

"All right. I have another burning question," he says, setting down his fork.

"That'll cost you."

"I think I can afford it." He pours me another glass of wine, and I smile and nod for him to ask away. "Worst date you've ever been on?"

I chuckle. "That's an easy one. It was when I was in high school. He was majorly obsessed with my dad and wouldn't stop asking about him. One night, when he dropped me off after a movie, he insisted on coming inside, and instead of kissing me good night or trying to sneak up to my room, he found my dad in front of the TV and spent the next hour and a half talking with him about hockey stats."

"Wait, was sneaking boys up to your room a regular thing for you?"

"I don't kiss and tell," I reply coyly, eyeing Jordie over the rim of my glass. "What about you? Or do all your dates end with a happily-ever-after?"

"Oh no," he says with a chuckle. "Your worst date sounds like a dream compared to my nightmares."

"Oh, really? Do tell."

"Well, you tell me what's worse. A date chatting up your dad, or a date puking up so much seafood in your bed that you have to get a new mattress?"

"Oh my God!" I say, almost snorting wine through my nose. "You're kidding. That's horrible!"

"I told her to avoid the seafood medley. But she insisted. She said it made her feel 'cultured.'"

We laugh, and I cover my face with my hands, groaning. "I'll never get that image out of my head."

"That makes two of us."

We laugh again and keep sharing horror stories from bad dates and weird interactions, and it isn't until our plates have long been cleared and my phone starts buzzing in my purse that I realize what time it is.

"Holy shit. How is it already nine thirty?"

Jordie gives me a skeptical look. "Is it past your bedtime or something?"

I chuckle. "Some of us have desk jobs that require us to get up early."

"Hey, for all you know, I could have a five a.m. workout scheduled in the morning."

My brows rise in question. "Do you?"

"Nah, tomorrow's the one day we get to sleep in," he says with a smile.

"I should probably call an Uber."

He frowns. "I'll drive you home. I only had one glass. And, hey, I promise you can trust me with your address." He raises his hands in surrender. "I'll keep my stalking to a minimum."

"Promises, promises." I roll my eyes and gather my things.

When we get into his truck, a wave of nerves washes over me. For a non-date, this is starting to feel a lot like a date. And I don't hate it.

Throughout the drive, I give him directions to my place, and we chat about our plans for the rest of the week. Jordie's is about what you'd expect— practice, power-play review, massage, and weight training. Mine's not quite as exciting, and mainly involves the same things I do every week—work, writing, volunteering, dinner with my dad, maybe going by to see my sister. In the back of my mind, I can't help but wonder when Jordie will find a time to pop up unexpectedly in my life again.

When we pull up in front of my place, I get butterflies in my stomach. *What the hell? Why am I suddenly so nervous?*

"Want me to walk you to your door?" Jordie asks softly.

"No, that's okay. It's a pretty safe neighborhood. I think I can manage."

He nods, and when I turn to look at him, I can't keep my gaze from drifting to his mouth.

"Thank you for rescuing me," I say, the fluttering in my stomach intensifying. "And for dinner. I really appreciate it."

"Anytime," he says, leaning his elbow on the center console, closing the distance between our faces.

Before I can talk myself out of it, I meet him halfway, and the moment our lips touch, it's like the butterflies turn into fireworks that immediately start exploding through every nerve ending. Everything else fades away—my car, my shitty day, the stupid rules I've created for myself. The only things that exist at this moment are Jordie and me, and what's happening between us.

And whatever it is? It's pretty freaking amazing.

His tongue touches mine, and I barely register the feel of his warm fingers sinking into the hair at the back of my neck, because *good Lord* . . . Jordie's tongue is doing all kind of magical things.

When we part, it feels like I'm in a daze.

He smiles. "That was—"

I cut him off by placing a finger on his lips. "Good night, Jordie," I say with a smile.

I slip out of his truck, turning to wave good-bye when I reach my door. He pulls away, and I walk inside, my heart still galloping like crazy against my ribs.

Because that kiss?

Was by far the best kiss I've ever had.

And no matter what I do for the rest of the night, I can't wipe that silly smile off my face.

CHAPTER EIGHT

Figuring It Out

Jordie

Tonight, I've been invited to have dinner at Grant and Ana's place, and since there's no way I'm turning down a home-cooked meal, I'm currently driving up I-5 North headed to their house.

They moved to the suburbs last summer into some crazy Mediterranean-style mansion in a gated community. Grant's basically living the dream—hot new wife, adorable baby daughter, huge luxurious estate. He's been through hell to get to this place in his life, and I'm nothing but happy for the guy.

When I arrive at the guard shack, I'm sent through after giving the security guard my name and flashing my driver's license. And when I roll up to the brick-paver-lined circular drive, I park my truck in front of the house. A little fountain splashes in the center of the driveway with artificially blue water cascading down into artfully arranged vessels.

Man, this place is over the top. But what else are you going to do with millions of dollars? You can't take it with you.

As I approach the front door, a small camera overhead pivots, recording my every move, so I'm not surprised when the door opens a few seconds later to reveal the entire family of three. A slightly disheveled-looking Grant, all six-foot-four of him in sweatpants and an Ice Hawks T-shirt; his petite wife, Ana, dressed in leggings and a sweatshirt; and their one-year-old daughter, Hunter, in a pair of light pink footie pajamas. Her hair is sticking up in about eight different directions, and she's gripping the leg of Grant's sweatpants with a hesitant look on her adorable little face.

"Hey." I grin at everyone. "Thanks for having me."

Grant thumps me once on the back while Ana pulls me in for a hug.

"Thanks for coming," she says.

"Brought you this," I say, handing her a bottle of the red wine I know she likes.

"You're so thoughtful." She smiles, meeting my eyes with a kind expression, then takes the bottle of wine and heads off for the kitchen.

Hunter tugs at her dad's sweatpants until he lifts her up in one arm and settles her against his ribs.

"She's getting big." I say, nodding to the blond-haired clone of Ana who shoves one chunky hand in her mouth.

He chuckles. "Yeah, she's teething now. And doesn't want to be put down either."

"Hmm. That must be challenging."

He shrugs. "You learn to do everything one-handed. You want anything to drink?" he asks as he leads me inside.

"Sure, I'll take a beer."

He heads into the huge chef's kitchen while I trail behind him, and pulls open a drawer that looks like a kitchen cabinet but is actually a beverage cooler. "Here, have a coconut water. It's good for rehydration."

"Oh … kay then. I guess I'll have a coconut water," I say on a chuckle.

Grant's eight years older than me, and he's always played the role of both captain and concerned older brother. I'd be lying if I said I didn't like it. Two years ago when I joined this team, I never expected to bond with him like I have. I figured I'd hit it off with the younger guys who were closer to my age, and I have. But Grant's the one who's become like a brother to me.

He murmurs something to Hunter, who is curled into his chest, and leads the way to the living room. Ana joins us, passing a pacifier to Hunter, which she promptly shoves into her mouth. She's pretty freaking cute.

"Any updates on that girl you're dating? Harper, right?" Grant asks as we settle onto one of the two big couches in his living room. Huge picture windows overlook the pool and an impressive green backyard beyond. There's a little playhouse with pink trim in the distance that I think is new.

I let out a sigh. "That depends . . . how much do you want to hear?"

"All of it, of course." He grins.

"Excuse me, I'm going to go throw up now,"

Ana says.

A chuckle dies on my lips when I realize, *oh shit*, she's serious. Ana bolts up from her seat and runs down the hall, where I overhear heaving sounds coming from the bathroom.

Fuck. "Is she okay?" I thought she was kidding—like the idea of my love life was nauseating enough to make her vomit.

"Ana's pregnant," Grant says with a soft grin.

"Again?" My eyebrows shoot up.

"Yes." He chuckles.

The last time Ana was pregnant, she was so sick that Grant called me in a panic, begging that I go to the pharmacy since he was too afraid to leave her side. Of course, I rushed to his place with all the necessary supplies.

"Is she all right? Should I leave?" I rise to my feet when Grant does.

"No, no." He waves me off. "Relax. I'm just going to check on her." He extends the baby toward me. "Hold Hunter for a minute?"

I panic slightly, my eyes widening. "Uh. Sure."

Not that I have much choice—same as with the

coconut water—which isn't half bad, by the way. Hunter is shoved into my arms before Grant leaves the room and heads toward where Ana is still making retching noises.

Jesus. That sounds awful.

"Hey." I grin at Hunter, bouncing her a little like I've seen Grant do.

Apparently, I'm a poor substitute for her dad, and she pulls out her pacifier to let out an unhappy little cry.

"It's okay. I'm your super-cool uncle Jordie, who will give you candy when you're older and won't rat you out when you break curfew. Don't cry, princess. We're cool, right?" I bounce her a little more.

She smiles. And then rips a loud fart.

I chuckle. Babies are awesome.

Grant returns a minute later. "Ana's all right. Come here, angel." He takes Hunter from me, and she nestles right into his chest like she belongs there.

Man, seeing Grant as a dad is still crazy. But it also just makes sense.

"Ana shouldn't be cooking, right?" I ask. "Not when she's feeling sick."

He shakes his head. "I've tried telling her that too. But, well, you'll see."

It turns out that he's right. No sooner than Ana rejoins us, she heads to the kitchen, retrieving items from the fridge for what appears to be tacos—ground bison, salsa, cheese, shredded cabbage.

I follow her, settling on a stool at the island. "Ana, please don't feel obligated to cook on my behalf. If you guys just want to chill tonight, I can go. Or if you're hungry, I'll run out and pick something up."

She gives me a dismissive wave. "Hush and park your butt right there. I'm fine with cooking. And I want to hear every single detail about this new girl who's got you all spun up."

My eyes widen, and I give her a nod.

"Told ya," Grant mutters under his breath.

As Ana cooks, Grant and I snack on chips and salsa at the island, while Hunter gnaws on an ice ring like it's her job. A string of drool dangles from her chin to her chest.

"Spill it, rookie. How are things going between you and Harper?" Grant asks.

My gaze darts between him and Ana, who is looking just as invested as her husband in finding out the nitty-gritty details of my lackluster dating life.

I suck in a deep breath before I speak. "I'm not sure, exactly. I think they're going okay."

If that kiss we shared last night is any indication, things are moving in the right direction. But still, I'm unsure. Harper is difficult to read, and she's definitely got a few walls up.

"How did you finally win over Ana?" I ask Grant.

Ana's eyes flash on mine, and a crooked smile curves her mouth.

Grant rubs one hand over the back of his neck, and he lets out a sigh. "It's not an easy story to tell. Are you looking for relationship advice, or what?"

It wasn't always this easy between them. Maybe I've brought up a sensitive topic. Who knows?

I nod. "Something like that."

Grant shifts. "Where is all this coming from?"

I fidget with the bottle in my hands, tightening the cap. "I watched this documentary about Japan. Have you ever heard of a hostess club?"

Grant gives me a confused look. "Nope."

"In these Japanese hostess clubs, men pay women for conversation. Women who aren't their wives or girlfriends. They hire these perfect strangers because they're desperate to connect with someone on an emotional level. It's not physical. Just conversation."

"Okay," he says slowly, still looking perplexed. "And . . . what? You're scared that's going to be you someday?"

I shrug, feeling more vulnerable than ever. "I don't know. Maybe."

"You're being weird, Jordie."

I exhale a sigh. "Yeah. Never mind."

Ana listens to our conversation while she cooks, occasionally making a soft noise of agreement or looking at me with a sympathetic expression.

After we eat, I help Grant clean up while Ana gives Hunter a bath. When Ana remerges from the hallway, it's without Hunter.

"I laid her down. She's already out," Ana says with a happy sigh.

I dry my hands on a kitchen towel and close their state-of-the-art dishwasher that's now full of our dinner dishes. "I have plans to grab a beer with a couple of the guys later. I'd better get going."

Grant nods. "Yeah. Thanks for stopping by."

"Thanks for dinner, Ana. It was amazing."

"You're welcome anytime. And don't worry so much, Jordie. You'll find the right girl."

I nod, even though I feel anything but certain.

• • •

After my dinner with Grant and Ana, I head home to drop off my truck. Then I call an Uber to take me to a restaurant to meet some of the guys for a much-deserved beer. Or three. We don't have a game for three more days, and I'm feeling relaxed and loose.

"Seriously, how'd you pull that one off, rookie?" one of my teammates asks when I tell them I cooked dinner for Harper the other night.

"Wait, Harper Allen, as in *Coach* Allen's daughter?" another asks.

I nod smugly. "Yup. And Coach is the one who gave me her number." I grab my forest-green Ice Hawks sweatshirt and tug it on over my head.

"Seriously, bro?" our starting goalie, Owen, asks with a confused expression.

"Seriously. He gave me her number and said I had a good head on my shoulders, and that he never saw me in the tabloids or with bunnies hanging all over me. I guess he trusts me with his daughter."

Owen gives me a side-eyed look. "Good thing he didn't come to Vegas last year."

"Eh, that's different." I shrug. "What happens in Vegas stays in Vegas. Well, unless you wake up married."

The guys chuckle.

That Vegas trip he's talking about is actually when I realized I wanted to make a change, that I want something more meaningful in my life than endless hookups.

"Just don't fuck this up with his daughter, rookie," Owen says. "Not unless you want to get traded to some team in Russia and be parked on the bench."

I grin. "Not planning on it."

The truth is, I like Harper, and after the other night, I think I might have finally gotten her to see I'm not the douchebag she originally took me for. And that kiss we shared? Holy fucking shit. It was hot.

"So, do you think she's finally going to go out with you, for real?" Owen asks around a mouthful of chicken wings.

"I hope so. I've only asked her out half a dozen times," I mutter, signaling the server for another beer.

Owen chuckles. "Maybe you should wait for her to ask you out. That way you'd know she was actually interested."

Teddy scoffs. "The guy does the asking. And the paying." He holds up one hand as I open my mouth to argue. "I know, I'm old school."

"Come on, TK. Think like a millennial. Things don't have to be so binary." Owen chuckles.

My teammates are trying to be helpful, but the more they talk, the more I tune them out.

One thing is glaringly obvious—I want my shot with Harper. And I won't stop until I get it.

• • •

Three hours later, I stumble out of an Uber and up to my front door. Even though I'm drunk and it's a bad idea, when I fall back onto my bed, I wrestle my phone out of my pocket and press the contact info of the woman who's been in my thoughts all night.

I shouldn't call her right now. I know that.

But loneliness is a powerful motivator. And I've never been very good at abstaining from the thing I'm not supposed to have.

"Hello?" She answers after the third ring, sounding confused.

"Harper. Heyyy," I rasp out.

"Jordie? It's late. What are you doing?"

"I went out with the guys tonight and just got home. And I was . . . thinking about you."

She pauses. "Are you drunk?"

"Uh, possibly." I chuckle into the phone.

She's quiet for a moment. "Is this a booty call?"

The idea of Harper coming over in the middle of the night to fuck me senseless is one my body doesn't hate, I'll be honest, even if I am interested in more with her.

My heart thumps against my ribs. "Would you say yes if it was?"

"Good-bye, Jordie." She doesn't sound impressed.

"No! Wait. It's not a booty call. I just wanted to talk to you. What are you doing?"

"Right now? I'm . . . uh . . . jotting down some notes for a piece I'm going to write tomorrow on the best fall vacations."

"Nice."

She makes a murmured sound that zings through me. "I'd be more fun if I actually got to go on one of these getaways. But it's not bad." When I'm quiet for a second, Harper says, "It's late, Jordie—"

"Go out with me. A real date this time," I blurt.

She sighs heavily into the phone. "You're not going to stop asking until I say yes, are you?"

"One date, that's all I'm asking for. And if you have an awful time, I promise I'll leave you alone. I swear it."

She's quiet, and *fuck*, I think for a second she's actually going to turn me down.

"I can't stop thinking about that kiss," I say softly into the silence.

She makes a breathy sound, and I have to press the heel of my hand over my cock to keep it from hardening.

Not now, fucker.

"One date, Jordie. That's all you get."

"Fuck yeah." I throw a fist pump into the air. "I mean . . . *cool*. Sounds good. I'll text you. We can figure out the day and time."

"Okay, that works. Night, Jordie."

"Night, Harper."

CHAPTER NINE

Good Times

Jordie

At six o'clock on Friday night, I'm parked in front of Harper's building.

Not sure which apartment is hers, I'm about to send her a text when she comes bounding down the stairs. I climb out of my truck, unable to wipe the smile from my face.

"Hey," she says, coming to a stop on the sidewalk before me.

My mouth twitches as I take her in. No one should look this good wearing ripped jeans and a sweatshirt, but Harper does. She really fucking does. It also amuses me that she didn't dress up for our date. Most girls would have just to impress me—even after I texted her and told her the date I've planned is casual. But, of course, Harper doesn't bend to anyone's expectations.

"Hope this is okay. I mean, the first time we met I was wearing a dress that made me look like a marshmallow, and since you still wanted a date, I figured there wasn't anything I could do to mess this up."

I laugh. "You look great. Come on."

Once we're inside my truck, I tug on the collar of my button-down shirt. "I feel overdressed."

Harper tries to pretend she's not checking me out, but I can feel her gaze on me from her side of the truck. "You're fine. So, where are we headed?"

"The square," I tell her, hoping it's the right move.

"Oh. They do outdoor ice skating there, right?"

I nod. "You skate?"

"I do," she says.

"Cool. They have a skating rink and awesome food trucks. It's really chill."

Harper's quiet for a second, and I can't tell if my date choice has surprised or annoyed her. Maybe she took me for the type of guy to plan a fancy night out, complete with an expensive restaurant, but that's really not me. Since Harper was fine letting me choose, and I'd rather be doing something physical . . . here we are.

"That sounds perfect, actually."

When we arrive, it takes a few minutes to find parking, and then I rent our skates and we lace up. Harper looks so damn cute in a pair of figure skates and that damn oversized sweatshirt, I'm grinning like an idiot when we take the ice. The hockey skates I've borrowed need to be sharpened, but there's no way I'm going to complain. Harper's finally here with me, and I'm a lucky man.

"Everything go okay with getting your car repaired?" I ask as we make a slow, smooth lap around the outdoor rink.

"Yeah, Miguel was great. How do you know him?"

"He's the friend of a friend. Great guy."

She nods. "Yeah, I had it back the next day, and the price was fair too."

I begged Miguel to squeeze her car in to make sure she had it in time for work the next day. When he didn't budge, I bribed him with tickets to our next home game, so I'm glad to see she's happy.

We pick up speed, dodging a group of giggling middle-school girls, and Harper flashes me a sassy look over one shoulder as she whizzes past me. By the time I catch up, I'm winded. When she's within reach, I grab her around the waist to tug her close, and she lets out a little squeal.

I'm about to make a joke, but when she turns her head and meets my eyes, the words stick in my throat. She's beautiful like this. Flushed cheeks, slightly breathless, and wearing a carefree smile.

I haven't known Harper long, but everything about her makes me want to know more. She's smart and sweet and funny. And she makes me work for it like no girl has before.

We skate for a little while longer until I spot a vendor selling gourmet hot cocoa nearby. "You want to take a break?"

She nods. "Let's do it."

We return our skates, and I walk over to get us drinks while Harper snags a nearby picnic table.

At the first sip, I realize I haven't had a mug of hot cocoa in years. It's really good. Rich and sugary, and my first thought is how sweet Harper's lips would taste right now if I kissed her. *Play it cool, Jordie.*

"So, tell me more about your job," I say instead.

She fills me in on the world of a being a freelance writer—she writes columns for several online magazines. I learn that her work has been featured in some of the biggest online publications, and a variety of popular women's magazines.

"It's flexible, and I like it," she says, finishing the last sip of her hot chocolate.

I nod, taking both of our paper cups over to the recycling bin. "Are you hungry?" I tip my head toward the half dozen food trucks parked down the street.

"Sure." She smiles, rising to her feet.

We both agree on pizza, and then take the oversized slices to a park bench, huddling close because now that the sun has gone down, it's getting chilly. Little white Christmas lights are strung up in the park, and even if I didn't exactly plan a romantic date, this somehow feels like one.

I pass Harper another napkin. "You mentioned you guys moved a lot growing up?"

She wipes her hands on the napkin. "All over the Pacific Northwest. Oregon, Washington, Northern California. We even lived in Montana for a year until my dad got fired."

"That must have been tough." I take another bite of pizza.

She nods. "I was in sixth grade, and I was already so used to the routine that I didn't even bother to make any friends that year. I knew we wouldn't be there long."

Damn. Tough doesn't even begin to describe it. I can picture Harper as a young girl, sitting alone at the lunch table with no one to talk to or pass notes with.

All night I've fantasized about kissing Harper, but suddenly that need vanishes, and the desire to comfort her takes its place. I want to wrap my arms around her and tell her it's okay. I want to fold her into my chest and just hold her.

Although my own childhood wasn't exactly all sunshine and rainbows, I still had some close friends growing up. I haven't told her about my past yet, and I'm not sure I will. It's something not a lot of people know about, and it's always hard to go back to that place and face those feelings all over again. I'm a pro at bottling up my emotions, because it's easier to bottle them up then to deal with them.

"What about you? What's your family like?" she asks, as if reading my mind.

Finishing my last bite of pizza, I wipe my mouth on a napkin. "That's kind of a tricky question to answer."

She gives me a concerned look as realization dawns that she might have just wandered into a touchy subject.

Just say it, Jordie. I clear my throat and draw a breath. "My dad committed suicide when I was thirteen."

Her hand lifts to her mouth. "Oh my God, Jordie."

I swallow the sudden lump of tension in my throat. I never tell people, never say the words out loud. A few guys on the team know my dad passed away, but I never say the s-word.

I nod and lick my lips. "Yeah. It was unexpected, and really, really tough. I was super close with my dad, so it was obviously devastating. We tried to carry on, but there was a huge hole. And then afterward, my mom kind of lost it. She went on this spiritual journey to find herself, and our relationship kind of fell apart after that. So I threw myself into hockey, and I guess the rest is history."

Harper meets my eyes with a somber expression. She seems to understand that although I play a sport I love for a living and command a multi-million-dollar salary doing it, I'd give it all up in a heartbeat for the shot at a normal family. Hockey was all I had. It helped me forget about all the hard stuff at home.

"I'm so sorry you had to go through that."

I nod. "Me too. I have an older sister. But she was already out of the house by then."

Harper nods her understanding.

For some reason, I keep right on rambling. "She's eight years older than me. We're closer now than we used to be growing up. She's a family therapist and owns her own practice downtown."

Harper reaches out, placing her hand over mine and squeezing. "That must come in handy."

I smile. "Sometimes. She definitely likes to give me advice, even when it's not asked for."

Harper suddenly stands, collecting our discarded paper plates and the pile of napkins from the park bench. "You want to get out of here? Grab a drink or something?"

"Absolutely." I stand, and rub her shoulders as

she shivers. "Sorry, I should have suggested that. You're probably getting cold, huh?"

She nods. "A little."

"We could go back to my place. I picked up more of that wine you liked."

Her mouth lifts in a half smile. "Is this just part of your grand plan to get me into your bed?"

I touch my heart in mock disbelief. "I would never."

She laughs. "Let's go."

Back at my place, I pour us each a glass of wine, which we take over to the couch. The conversation earlier turned heavy, and I'm hoping to lighten the mood.

"So, did you go to college for writing?"

She nods. "Yes. I graduated with an English degree and wasn't sure what I wanted to do. Most of my advisors suggested teaching, but I couldn't see myself standing at the front of a classroom for eight hours a day. I wanted to be actually writing, you know?"

"Yeah, that makes sense." I nod.

She takes another sip of wine and crosses one

leg over the other. Through the rip in her jeans, I can see part of her thigh, just above her knee. It's really only four inches of skin, but the effect on me is instantaneous.

My cock stirs, and I will it down. *Not now, fucker.*

"What about you?" she asks. "Did you go to college?"

I don't answer for a second because I'm distracted by her mouth. Smooth of me, I know.

"I actually had a couple of scholarship offers from Division One schools, but I was drafted straight out of high school, and that seemed like the better move. I played for two years in the minors before being called up to the pros." I pause to smile at her. "I've got to say, I kind of love that you don't know all of this already. Usually when I go out with a girl, she's already googled the shit out of me and knows every detail before I even open my mouth."

"I'm not like most girls." Harper's voice is low, and her eyes glitter as they search mine.

"Believe me, I've noticed. And I like that a whole hell of a lot."

Harper licks her lips, her teeth dragging across her plump lower lip in a way that makes my pants tighten.

"Come here." My voice is deep and raspy.

I take our wineglasses and set both on the table. Then I thread my fingers into the hair at the nape of her neck and guide her toward me. She relaxes, letting me draw her closer until her soft mouth presses to mine.

Harper might have been shy about going out with me, but there's nothing timid about the way she kisses. She puts her whole body into it, leaning close until her soft breasts press against my chest, and her knees touch mine.

When my lips part, her tongue makes a greedy pass against mine, and I can't help the low, growling noise that escapes the back of my throat. She tastes so good, like red wine and chocolate, but it's not enough. I want to taste her everywhere.

My mouth travels from hers, down to her jaw, along the column of her throat with soft sucking kisses. She shivers and lets out a need-filled groan.

"Jordie," she murmurs, threading her fingers into my hair to move my mouth back to hers.

My body is screaming at me to get us naked and into my bed, but I ignore it, forcing myself to go slow and enjoy her kisses. And believe me, I am enjoying it. The wild hammering of my heart, the fiery arousal thrumming through my veins, the rock-hard dick trying to escape my pants? Yeah . . . kissing Harper is way better than I could have ever imagined.

Fastening her mouth to mine, Harper crawls into my lap until she's straddling me on my couch. I grip her ass in both hands and groan when she works her pelvis over my erection.

The confident strokes of her tongue, the eager rock of her hips, it all feels so fucking good.

I ease one hand under the hem of her sweatshirt, brushing my knuckles over the soft skin of her lower back. Her fingertips trace the muscles in my chest and shoulders, and she squirms in my lap, practically riding me. I let out a deep groan.

With a fortifying breath, she pulls back to meet my eyes. "We shouldn't be doing this."

"Why not?" I say smoothly, shifting to ease the pressure on my groin.

Her eyes are dark with arousal and her cheeks are flushed, and I absolutely love knowing it's me who put that look there. "I don't know . . . aren't there guidelines or something? First date equals first kiss, but like, nothing below the belt?"

"I don't know." I press my lips to her neck.

"Jordie, be real. You do know." She pushes playfully against my chest.

I meet her eyes again and suck in a deep breath. "Do you want the truth?"

She nods. "Of course."

I'm probably about to ruin everything that's beginning between us and make her flee from my apartment, but I can't help it. I have to be honest. "The truth is I have no idea what I'm doing, and I never learned the rules."

She gives me a skeptical look, tucking her hair behind one ear. "What does that mean? That because you're a professional athlete, the rules never applied to you?"

I nod, feeling sheepish.

A little wrinkle appears between her arched eyebrows. "Meaning . . . what? You're used to having sex on the first date?"

"I'm not even used to having to go on a date in

order to have sex. But, yeah, something like that."

"Jordie!"

"You wanted honesty." I shrug, a little embarrassed, but I won't lie to her or hide my past. Girls have always been readily available to enjoy. "I'm sorry if I sound like a douche."

She bites on her plump bottom lip, and I wait for her to tell me she's done and that she doesn't want to see me again. But she shocks the shit out of me when she says, "Okay, well, that's not how this is going to work."

"I know," I say, touching her cheek. I love the rosy flush that still lingers there. I also love that she's still sitting in my lap and sounding like she wants to give this a shot with me. "Let's make up our own rules, okay?"

"Okay." She nods, a determined look crossing her features. "Nothing inside the pants."

"Wear a skirt next time," I say, teasing, and she gives me a pointed look. "I'm kidding. We can go at whatever pace you're comfortable with."

"Are you sure?"

"Positive. With one tiny caveat. I haven't manscaped, so if you're set on this happening tonight, it's enter at your own risk inside my boxer briefs. A guy needs more advance warning."

"You're unbelievable." She chuckles, and the pink on her cheeks deepens.

"I'm unbelievably attracted to you. And I'm seriously fine with taking things slow."

She licks her lips. "Thanks, Jordie. So, you seriously didn't expect anything to happen between us tonight?"

"I swear it. I'm just happy you're here with me, and that you gave me a shot to take you out."

It's the complete truth. The guys teased me at the gala, asking what I wanted out of this, and if I really saw myself settling down with someone. At the time, I brushed off their comments.

But now? Sitting here with this gorgeous girl, watching her face light up as we talk, feeling her heartbeat pounding against mine? I try to remember what's so great about being single.

The lonely nights? Eating dinner alone? Maybe if I was lucky, taking home a fan to sleep with who I'd have to kick out in the morning while trying not to seem like a total dick.

Watching most of my teammates find their other half, settle down, and get married, it does something to a guy. Maybe the idea of love isn't so bad. Monogamy certainly has its place, and I can actually see myself wanting something like that with Harper.

She definitely isn't the kind of girl you share with another dude. There's nothing casual about her. I want her all to myself.

Harper is the kind of girl who'd wait up for you after a game, who'd rub your shoulders if they were sore, and cook you lasagna simply because you said it was your favorite food. The kind of girl who'd ask you insightful questions about the book you're reading. The kind of girl who volunteers her time to help those in need. The kind of girl you want to protect and cherish forever.

Okay, Jodie. Get it the fuck together.

Harper licks her lips and smiles at me. "I'm happy I'm here too."

I lean in and kiss her again, loving the way her talented tongue traces mine while her hips continue to taunt me. Each kiss is endless, blurring and blending into the next.

It's with great effort that I pull my mouth from hers. "We'd better stop now. I might embarrass myself if we don't."

Harper climbs from my lap while I not-so-discreetly adjust myself.

She stands and takes her wineglass to the kitchen as I follow. "I had fun tonight."

"I did too," I say, wrapping her in a hug beside my sink. Apparently, I have a hard time keeping my hands to myself when she's near.

I drive her home, and by the time we reach her building, I'm plotting ways to get her to agree to go out with me again, but I'm also trying to play it cool. When I park by the curb, she turns to face me.

"Night, Jordie."

I lean close and draw her in for one last kiss. "Good night, Harper."

With the taste of her still on my lips, I watch until she's safely inside her apartment building's entrance, then I head toward home.

But when I arrive back at my place, I'm no more settled than I was before. I'm still worked up. Still horny.

And when I crawl into bed, and my right hand drifts down underneath the elastic of my boxer briefs, it's Harper that I'm thinking about. Her mouth, and those breathy sounds she made when we kissed. The feel of her hand on mine on that park bench. As I jack myself in long, steady strokes, I realize that I've never been this into a girl before.

I'm falling hard and fast, and there's not a damn thing I can do about it.

CHAPTER TEN

Daydreaming

Harper

The kettle whistles, snapping me out of the daze I've been in for the past fifteen minutes. Taking the kettle off the burner, I give my head a quick shake, trying to refocus my brain on what I should be thinking about—the article I'm supposed to be writing.

The last thing I ever expected was for my date with Jordie to go so well. Like *really* well. Like *can't stop thinking about it and getting hot and bothered* well. Which is a huge problem, given the fact that I don't date hockey players, even though I went on a date with one last night. But that doesn't count. I was just fulfilling my duties as the fill-in ice princess, right? He won the date fair and square, and who am I to go against decades of tradition?

Crap. I'm not even convincing myself with that logic. Nope, I'm just a phony who can't stick to her own rules.

I like Jordie. Despite the fact that he's a hockey player. And despite the fact that I really, really need to buckle down and figure out how to write this damn piece on tech law.

This is one of those instances where working a normal nine-to-five in an office would come in handy. I could chat with my favorite coworker by the water cooler about the crazy-hot make-out sesh I had with Jordie last night, get it all out of my system, and move on with the rest of my day. But working in a home office just a few feet away from my bedroom makes that really hard to do. Plus, now I'm imagining what might happen in said bedroom the next time Jordie takes me home.

After grabbing my favorite mug from the shelf, I pour myself a generous cup of green tea with a little bit of honey. It's my favorite writing drink when it's cold out, because it's warm and comforting but still gives me a little boost of caffeine to keep me going.

I pad back to my office and settle into my chair, pressing a random key on the keyboard to wake up my computer. As soon as the screen changes from black to my screensaver (an adorable picture of my dad playing tea party with my nieces), a notice pops up in the corner of my screen, reminding me that I'm scheduled to volunteer at the animal shelter in an hour.

Shit, I totally forgot. Damn Jordie, getting in my head and making me forget things.

I get as much onto the page as I can before making a mad dash to my bedroom, change into my dog-kennel-appropriate clothes, and book it to the shelter. No one will say anything if I'm a few minutes late, but I made a commitment, and I don't want to leave anyone in the lurch.

"Hey, Trisha," I say, out of breath as I jog past the girl at the front desk. "Sorry I'm late."

"Harper, it's like two minutes after four," she says, smiling and twirling the end of her ponytail.

"Well, it feels like I'm late."

"You're too hard on yourself."

I respond with a halfhearted chuckle and peel my coat from my body, which is a little sweatier than I'd like to admit.

"Hey, is your friend coming again? The cute one?" Her eyes dance mischievously.

"Oh, uh, that's a good question. I don't know. Probably not."

I try to sound cool and casual and collected, but I totally forgot that Trisha knows who Jordie is. And that she's seen his face. I'm not surprised that she thinks he's cute—he's freaking gorgeous. But I'd be lying if I said that hearing her talk about him like that didn't make me bristle a little.

Trisha shrugs, tossing her ponytail over her shoulder. "Byron's already getting started on the kennels."

"Great. Thanks."

I breeze by her, making a quick stop in the staff room to drop my purse and jacket before making my way through the building to the kennels.

It's funny to think that two weeks ago when I was here, so was Jordie. I feel a little bad now about how harsh I was with him. But that was *before*.

Things feel different between us after our date, now that he's opened up and told me about his family. I think I trust him now, even though there's still a little voice in the back of my head telling me not to, reminding me that one good date or not, he's still a pro athlete. And I've had a front-row seat to witness the kind of lifestyle those guys live.

When I make it to the back of the building, I find Byron herding the last of the rescues from their kennels into the playroom. As much as we love playing with the pups, it's a lot easier to clean their little homes when they're not in them.

"Sorry I'm late," I say, pulling the cleaning supplies out of the nearby closet.

"You're late? I thought I got here early," Byron says, scrunching his face up and adjusting his wire-rimmed glasses.

"It's been a weird day, okay?"

Byron nods and pats me on the shoulder. "Ah, that time of the month?"

"I'm sorry, what?" I step away and shoot him an incredulous look, but he just stares blankly back at me.

"Are we not at that point yet? Damn, I'm sorry. I'm just trying to be sympathetic."

I shake my head and get back to cleaning. Byron's weird and sometimes a little offensive, but at the end of the day, he's harmless. Not that that keeps me from calling him out on his bullshit.

"I don't know that we'll ever be at a point where you can feel free to ask about my menstrual cycle."

He scrubs his beard, looking apologetic. "I'll clean Frito's kennel to make it up to you."

My eyes go wide. Frito is a lovable hundred-pound mutt who has a bad habit of shitting the bed and rolling around in it. Not to mention peeing when he's nervous—which is pretty much all the time. You can always tell which kennel is his by the smell alone, and every week we roshambo to see who'll be stuck with it. So the fact that Byron's *offering* to clean it is pretty major.

I collect myself, straightening and giving him a joking, icy glare. "I suppose that punishment will do."

His face falls. "Aw, really? I was hoping you'd accept the gesture and tag team it with me."

"No way. You're the one who was stupid enough to offer."

He sighs loudly and lugs his bucket and spray bottles down the hall a few yards away from me, pretending to throw up when he reaches Frito's kennel.

"Hey, maybe you can call your friend to come

help me," he says between gags.

"My friend?"

"Yeah, you know, that guy that unclogged the women's toilet a couple weeks ago. He did a pretty good job, actually. I don't think that was his first clogged toilet."

I sigh. *Jordie.* I knew who Byron was talking about. I was just trying to buy myself a few seconds of uninterrupted reminiscing.

"Oh, right. I, uh, think he's a little busy." A little busy clouding my thoughts with memories of his tongue when I'm trying to get some real work done.

"What could be more important than this?" Byron holds a bottle full of bright blue disinfectant in the air.

The feel of Jordie's hard body underneath mine. The strain behind his zipper. The fact that I can't stop thinking about how badly I want his hands all over me again.

Jeez, Harper. Focus.

"Um, he's probably at practice or a workout or something."

"Oh, is he in, like a softball league or something?"

I snort. I can just see the look on Jordie's face if he were here to hear that. "No, actually, he's a hockey player."

"Oooh, I see. Still have all his teeth?"

I have to keep myself from sighing out loud at the thought of Jordie's kind, warm smile. And how quickly it can be replaced by something steamier, something dark and full of desire.

"Yep, they're all there."

"Is there some adult hockey league I don't know about?"

This time I burst out laughing. "Ever heard of the NHL?"

"Holy shit, he's a Hawk?"

That's more like the reaction I was expecting. I can't imagine what Byron would do if he found out my dad is the coach.

"Even more impressive that he has all his teeth, right?"

"I can't believe one of the Seattle Ice Hawks fixed a clogged toilet in the same animal shelter as me. My friends are going to shit themselves when

I tell them."

Byron keeps blabbering on about how he can't believe how crazy life is, and it doesn't take long for me to tune him out and immediately start thinking about my date with Jordie. Yet again.

I don't know if I care anymore that Jordie's a hockey player. The fact that he's willing to take things slow feels like a good sign to me, like maybe he's not like every other douchebag, overly cocky player I've met. And the way he opened up to me about his dad? That has to mean something, right? He's different. I can feel it. Just like I can still feel his lips against mine. And his body. And his hands running over my skin, ready to slip under my panties—

"Harper, what are you doing?" Byron yells.

I snap out of my fantasy, only to find that I'm about to reach my hand into a vat of pure bleach. Quickly pulling my hand away, I try to shrug casually at Byron, who's looking at me like I just ate a live tarantula in front of him.

"I got the buckets mixed up, okay?"

He makes a tsking sound and shakes his head. "You're gonna really get yourself hurt one of these days, you know that?"

That's exactly what I'm afraid of.

CHAPTER ELEVEN

The Truth Hurts

Jordie

After a team skate and then lunch, I called my sister's therapy practice and spoke to the receptionist to see if I could snag a few minutes of Tiffany's time. I was told she had exactly twenty-six minutes until her next appointment arrived, so I hightailed it over there, and now here I am.

"There's my favorite sister," I say, rounding the corner to enter Tiffany's office as the receptionist waves me in. Apparently, I now only have fourteen minutes left.

She rolls her eyes as she looks up from her laptop. "I'm your only sister, jackass."

Tiffany stands, teetering in her high heels, and gives me a one-armed hug. Then I plop myself down onto the chair in front of her desk.

I refuse to sit on the couch in her office. Doing so, I've learned in the past, is an open invitation for her to psychoanalyze me. Not that anything will stop her, really. After four years in undergrad and then three more in grad school studying psychology, it's in Tiffany's blood. And she's damn good at what she does. She has a nose for sniffing out problems before you even realize you've opened yourself up.

"Do you want a cup of coffee?"

"Sure." I shrug.

She tips her chin toward the Keurig machine on the cabinet on the other side of her office. "Help yourself."

I chuckle and get up to make myself a mug of coffee. "Have you talked to Mom lately?" I ask as I select a pod of dark roast and place it into the machine.

"Nope. Last I heard she was working on becoming a Pilates instructor. That was a month or so ago, though, so who the hell knows."

Mom could be off living in Guam for all we know. I only hear from her a few times a year, and it's usually when she needs a favor.

I grab my mug of coffee and slide back into the chair in front of Tiffany. "How have you been?"

She grins like she knows something I don't. "I've been great. Don and I are planning a getaway this spring. But since you're here, that means you need something, so let's just cut to the chase."

I frown and blow on my coffee. "Who says I need something? Can't I just come visit my big sister on a Wednesday afternoon?"

Tiffany scoffs. "Come on, I know you better than that. The last time you showed up here during the middle of the day was because you thought you were going to get cut from the team, and you were freaking out."

For the record, I wasn't freaking out. But, yeah, Tiffany's advice calmed me down, so I could focus on playing the best I could, which in turn got Coach off my back. "Fine. I met someone."

Tiffany grins. "Ohhh, girl problems. The best kind. Lay it on me." She rubs her hands together excitedly.

I chuckle. "You're the actual worst. You know that, right?"

She scoffs. "Hey, I'm here to help. I normally charge two hundred dollars an hour for this kind of help, but as my only sibling, you get it for free."

"Lucky me," I mutter.

"So, who is she?"

My mouth lifts in a smile without my permission. "She's actually my coach's daughter."

Tiffany gasps. "Mmm, scandalous and forbidden. I'm surprised you're okay with that scenario. Isn't that like mixing church and state?"

She knows how seriously I take my hockey career, but it's not like that.

I shake my head. "Not really. Coach is cool with it. He's actually the one who gave me her number."

Tiffany's eyebrows pinch together. "Okay, then what's the problem?"

"She doesn't date hockey players. Told me this whole story about how growing up with a coach as her father ruined the sport for her. Always having to move when he got transferred, always coming in second to whatever team he was working for."

I don't tell my sister about Harper's parents' divorce—again, likely due to his hockey schedule—

or how she confided in me that she didn't bother to make a single friend in the sixth grade because she knew she wouldn't be there long enough.

Tiffany nods. "Makes sense that she'd be leery, then. Childhood pain is always the hardest to heal from. So, she won't go out with you, and now your ego is crushed?"

I half expected Tiffany to make fun of me, but instead she's looking at me with a solemn expression. "Sorta. We actually did go out, once officially. And a few other times I just happened to be at the same place as her."

She laughs. "Stalker, much?"

"Basically." I chuckle. "But I was desperate for a shot. This girl is literally perfect."

"No girl is perfect, Jordie."

I shake my head. "This girl is. Smart. Pretty. Funny as hell. She doesn't hesitate to call me out. I guess I never knew it, but I like that."

Tiffany nods. "Most of the girls you've been out with worship the ground you walk on, so it's only natural you'd be drawn to someone who makes you work for their affection."

"I don't know about all that, but I definitely feel

a connection with her. Like I haven't with anyone before."

She weighs my words, tapping a pen against her pursed lips. "This isn't like you."

"Believe me, I know." I never go chasing after women. Normally, they come to me, and I enjoy what's offered until it runs its course, and it always does. But with Harper, the more time I spend with her, the more time I want.

Tiffany taps her pen against her lower lip, still watching me. "So, when you guys did go out, how was it?"

"Amazing. She's so chill. We both opened up. Laughed a lot. And did I mention she's gorgeous?"

Tiffany chuckles. "Okay, Romeo, I get the picture. So you're into her."

Understatement. "Yeah, I am. I just don't think she feels the same way."

"Because of the whole no-hockey-player rule? Or because she doesn't enjoy your company as much as you do hers?"

I consider this, scratching at the stubble on my chin. "I'm not sure. Maybe a mix of both?"

My sister leans back in her chair, still watching me.

I try not to fidget and take another sip of my coffee. "Just tell me what you're thinking, already. It's obvious you've got an opinion."

Because, let's be honest, when does my sister *not* have an opinion?

Don't wear your hair like that, Jordie.

Brown shoes don't match black pants, Jordie.

Girls don't like dick pics, Jordie.

Her advice has always been endless.

Tiffany licks her lips. "I do have an opinion. I just doubt you're going to like it."

I scoff. "When has that ever stopped you before?"

"Jackass." She smirks. "Well, first I think you've always been desperate for female approval."

"I have not."

She pauses, meeting my gaze with a serious stare. "Let me finish. All the women, all the meaningless flings . . . yeah, you have. You needed that affection and reassurance, even if it was in the form of no-strings sex."

"I'm not talking about sex with my sister. 'Bye, Tiff." I start to rise from my seat.

"Wait. I'm not talking about sex either. Will you just listen to me for a second?"

Settling back into my seat, I glance at my watch. "Sure. You've got four minutes."

She rolls her eyes. "You and I both know you were a little wild during your adolescence and early twenties."

"Fine," I say, raising my hands in defeat. Plus, there's really no use in denying it. My sister knows I went through a slutty stage. "I concede the argument. Your point?"

"My point is that you're growing up. You're older now. You recognize that casual flings aren't enough, and want something deeper now. And for whatever reason, you've set your sights on this woman."

I nod. "Maybe."

"Definitely. And you don't find it a little odd that the one woman you want to give your heart to is emotionally unavailable? Just like Mom was?"

"Fuck, Tiff." *Why does everything have to come back to our mother?* "Honestly, I hate when you psychoanalyze me."

She swallows, her expression softening. "I know you do, Jordie. But I also know that sometimes when you come and see me, you need to hear it, okay? I'm only trying to help. I love you. Very much."

"I love you too," I say begrudgingly.

"Have you slept with her yet?" she blurts out next.

I'm not sure what that has to do with anything, but I exhale and shake my head. "No."

Tiffany's eyes widen. "Okay, that's interesting."

I shift in my seat. "I'm not sure how that's relevant . . ."

She grins knowingly. "Unconsciously, you're trying to show her that she means more to you than just a hookup. It's a good thing, Jordie. My advice would be that you wait to have sex until your relationship is on more solid footing. Sex complicates things."

A smirk tugs on my lips. "Pretty sure it doesn't."

She shakes her head. "Not the kind of sex you've been having. But sex with a person you care about? Sharing your body with someone you want a future with? Yeah, it's a much bigger deal."

I clear my throat, suddenly feeling unsure if I should have come here today, if I should have gotten Tiffany's advice at all. Because now I feel even less confident about things than when I walked in.

Her intercom buzzes, and the receptionist announces the arrival of her next appointment.

I stand, grabbing my coffee mug. "I'd better go."

"I'm sorry if that wasn't what you wanted to hear today," Tiffany says, a little less pointedly, her warm eyes meeting mine.

Rinsing my mug in the little sink across the room, I glance at her over my shoulder and force a smile onto my lips. "It's all good."

"Just try not to get your heart broken, okay?" Her tone is sincere and a little unsteady.

I laugh, but the sound is hollow, because there's a whole lot of truth to Tiffany's words. "I'll try my best."

"That's all we can do."

"Good chat," I say dryly.

Tiffany laughs, and I do too, despite my discomfort. "You're very lovable, Jordie. It's just going to take the right girl."

I nod, understanding exactly what she's insinuating. The right girl being someone who doesn't have a vendetta against hockey players.

When I leave my sister's office, I head straight to the gym at the training facility. I tell myself that I want to burn off a little extra energy before heading home, but the workout I subject myself to feels more like I'm punishing myself for something. And when I check my phone on the drive home, I still haven't heard from Harper.

Tiffany's words about Harper being emotionally unavailable ring through my head on a constant loop, and my mood plummets faster than a time clock in the final seconds of a game. But this isn't a game to me. This could be the real thing. I just need to make Harper see it that way.

Although, according to my sister, this could all end in disaster. Not just could—probably will.

Good times.

CHAPTER TWELVE

Finding the Strength

Harper

There are times in our lives when something happens that changes everything. Something that shocks you, that wakes you up and shakes you out of a funk you didn't even realize you were in. And suddenly it's clear that nothing will ever be the same again.

Like when you find yourself sobbing in the waiting area of a hospital, and no one will tell you what happened or what's going on, and it feels like your entire world is shattering around you.

That's what's happening to me right now.

I've been sitting in the same green waiting-room chair for ten minutes, but it feels like I've been here for hours. My dad's in the emergency room. And I have no idea why, not that that keeps my brain from immediately jumping to the worst conclusions. We knew his heart issues were getting serious, but I still didn't think this is where we would end up. And what if it's something even worse?

I bury my face in my hands, trying to keep my mind from totally spinning out.

"Harper?" My sister comes rushing in through the sliding glass doors.

Just hearing her voice makes me feel like someone has thrown me a life preserver. I gasp and call her name, and Faith runs across the room to meet me, her eyes red and wild. We throw our arms around each other, and a fresh round of tears stream down my cheeks. We hold on tight until we both start to calm down, and when we pull away, one look at her face shows me exactly what mine must look like.

"Where are the girls?" I ask.

"With their dad. I didn't want to scare them." My sister rubs my arm like she always does when I'm upset. Like a mom does. "Have you heard anything? Where is he?"

I shake my head and sniffle loudly. "They've

barely told me anything. One of the players called me and said Dad was in an ambulance and on his way here. He collapsed at practice. That's all I know. I've tried talking to some of the nurses, but all they keep saying is a doctor will come talk to us once they know what's going on."

My words come out all at once, in the same breath, and hearing it all out loud suddenly makes it even more real. My eyes well up with tears for what feels like the hundredth time in the past hour. I'm surprised there's any liquid left in my body.

As if on cue, a balding doctor wearing small wire-framed glasses comes striding through the door to the waiting room, his white coat billowing around him. "Allen? Anyone here for Mark Allen?"

"Yes, over here!" I say, louder than I meant to, but I don't care. My dad's in the hospital. I'll freaking scream if I have to.

The doctor nods and walks toward us, his expression blank and unreadable.

"He's our dad," Faith says, slipping her arm around my waist.

"Your father had a heart attack," the doctor says matter-of-factly.

I whimper, but Faith stays silent, bracing herself—bracing both of us—for what might come next.

"All things considered, it was mild," he says. "We put him on blood thinners and beta-blockers. He'll be all right, but we'll be keeping him overnight for observation, and so we can run some tests to check for lasting damage."

Faith breathes a sigh of relief, and I break down in tears again.

I keep repeating the doctor's words in my head. *He'll be all right. He'll be all right. He'll be all right.*

"Do you know what pharmacy your father uses? We also have some paperwork to fill out . . ."

I tune the doctor out as my sister takes over answering his questions and dealing with the paperwork. Faith has a family of her own now, so lately, I've been the one handling Dad's health stuff. But in this moment, I can't handle anything.

I'm flooded with a rush of emotions . . . relief, frustration, sadness, anger, guilt. I was the one who was supposed to be taking care of our dad. I was the one who was supposed to be helping him manage this whole heart thing. And I blew it. I failed him. All of this is my fault.

"Hey, Harper, do you have Dad's social security number anywhere?" Faith turns to me, in full business mode, and her expression softens the second she sees the look on my face. "Oh, sweetie, Dad's going to be just fine."

She places a hand on my shoulder, but this time, I shrug her off. I don't deserve to be comforted. It's my fault that we're here. That he's here. I should have been taking better care of him.

"Can we see him?" I stare at the doctor, whose expression is still professional and detached.

"I'm afraid visiting hours just ended. Your father is in good hands. You can come see him in the morning."

I scoff and shake my head. "Are you kidding me? My dad had a heart attack, and you're not going to let us see him? Who the hell do you think—"

"Harper?"

Before I can finish telling this jackass of a doctor exactly how I feel, a voice cuts me off. A voice that comforts and surprises me all at once. Jordie's voice.

I turn around to find Jordie walking toward me,

his expression stern and panicked. I rush to meet him halfway, and he wraps me in his arms, holding me as fresh tears well up in my eyes.

"What are you doing here?" I step back to get a better look at him. He clearly came straight from practice, based on the collar of his base layer peeking out from underneath his T-shirt, and sweat beading along his hairline. Even sweaty and flushed, he's overwhelmingly attractive.

"I came as soon as I heard. I was running drills with the forwards when I heard the other guys start yelling. Someone said something about Coach and calling 9-1-1 . . . It all happened so fast, but I knew you would be here. I wanted to come and make sure you're okay."

"Thank you," I whisper, staring up at his worried blue eyes.

"Is he going to be okay?" Jordie looks over at the doctor, who's still talking to my sister.

"He had a mild heart attack," I say. "They're putting him on a bunch of medications, but Doctor Jackass over there said he'll be all right."

"Doctor Jackass?" Jordie gives me a curious look.

"He won't let us see him."

"That's bullshit."

"That's what I said. But my sister seems to think we should listen to him." I jerk my chin in her direction, and Jordie nods, his jaw clenched.

Faith thanks the doctor, and when he leaves, probably to go disappoint another patient's family.

After she joins us, I make quick introductions, and she says, "He said Dad's going to be just fine. With a few small lifestyle changes and some new medications, we can make sure this never happens again."

"He had a heart attack. I don't think *fine* is the word I would use to describe him right now," I grumble.

She gives me a cautious look. "All things considered, I'd say he's doing pretty well."

"Look, I was doing my best, okay? I cut down the number of times he has red meat a week. I stocked his fridge with more vegetables. I told him to drink less beer and more sparkling water. I don't know what else you want me to do." I cross my arms, tossing my ponytail over my shoulder.

"Harper, no one's blaming you."

Solemnly, I nod. She might not blame me, but it doesn't change the fact that right now, I feel like crap.

"You want some company?" Jordie asks, touching my shoulder.

I meet his eyes. "What'd you have in mind?"

He shrugs. "I could drive you home. Hang out for a while, if you don't feel like being alone."

I take a second to think it over. I certainly didn't expect him to show up here, but his offer is a generous one. I can't imagine going home alone right now. All I'd do is worry. A distraction could be a good thing, and Jordie would be the perfect distraction.

"Sure, that'd be great."

As I follow him to his truck, I realize Jordie's right. I'm in no state to drive. Besides, I'll be back first thing in the morning, and I can get my car then.

We drive to my place in silence, the radio playing some song about heartbreak, and Jordie places a hand reassuringly on my knee. I inhale deeply and try to stay calm.

When we get to my place, Jordie insists on running me a bath.

"You really don't have to," I say, self-consciously running my fingers through my knotted ponytail.

"You're freezing. This will make you feel better."

He's right. I didn't realize how cold I was until he said it. He pours a couple of capfuls of my body wash into the water, and bubbles begin to form on the surface.

"Are you hungry?" he asks.

It's dinnertime, I realize, so I nod. "A little."

Jordie gives me another kind look. "I'll get you something to eat. Please take your time and try to relax," he says, leaving me to undress and climb into the tub.

The second my toes hit the hot water, I let out a sigh, easing the rest of my stiff, chilled body in. Normally a shower person, I haven't taken a bath in at least six months, and after the emotional turmoil of the day, it's exactly what I needed. Jordie was right.

Twenty minutes later, he softly knocks on the bathroom door. "You okay, Harper?"

"Yeah. I'll be out in a minute."

"Take your time," he says. "There's soup when you're ready."

I smile and rise from the tub. After I pull the drain and towel off, I get dressed in a pair of gray flannel pajamas. A brief thought about dressing in something a little nicer to impress Jordie crosses my brain, but I push the thoughts away. Tonight is about comfort, and I don't need to impress this man. He's here because he was worried about me.

When I emerge with damp hair, Jordie is standing in my kitchen.

"Hey," I say softly.

He turns around and my breath catches in my throat. The look of concern in his deep blue eyes renders me momentarily speechless.

"Come here," he says, opening his arms.

I take a few steps forward, and then Jordie is pulling me into his wide chest, hugging me like his life depends on it.

"He's going to be okay, Harper," he says softly against my hair.

I nod and squeeze my eyes closed. I hope to God he's right.

When Jordie releases me, he busies himself in my kitchen, gathering a bowl of steaming soup for me and a sleeve of crackers I didn't even know I had, and carries everything into the living room. I follow him, feeling out of place in my own apartment. I'm really glad he's here. Jordie settles onto the couch while I take my first spoonful of soup.

"This is good. Thank you."

"Anytime." He nods, watching me closely while I sip one slow spoonful after another.

When I finish, I lean back into the couch, covering myself with a fuzzy throw blanket.

"Are you tired?" he asks, still gazing at me.

"Not really."

He moves closer. "Want to watch a movie?"

I shake my head. "I don't think I could concentrate on a movie right now. Maybe we can just talk?"

Jordie seems to understand that means he should talk and I'll listen, because a second later, he shifts and launches into a story about how he went to visit his sister the other day.

"Yeah? How was that?"

He shrugs. "It was all right. I told her about you."

This pulls a smile out of me. "You did?"

He nods. "Of course. Although, maybe I shouldn't have, because then I had to listen while she doled out her signature tough-love advice."

I don't ask about what that advice entailed, partly because it's not my business, and partly because Jordie doesn't look like he's ready to talk about it.

"I wanted to thank you . . . for opening up." I meet his eyes with a look of admiration. "For telling me about your family, about your dad. That couldn't have been easy for you."

Jordie swallows and gives me a tight nod. "I don't usually tell people. But I trust you, Harper."

"You can," I say, curling my legs beneath me. "I won't tell anyone."

"I know," he says, his tone certain.

Our silence is interrupted by Jordie's phone, which vibrates with a series of texts. He pulls it from his pocket and scans the screen.

"Everything okay?" I ask, perching on the

couch next to him.

"Yeah, just the guys in the group chat. Everyone's worried about your dad." He taps quickly at the screen with his thumbs. "I'm letting them know he's going to be just fine."

I swallow past a lump in my throat. *God, I hope so*. I don't know what I'd do without my dad. Ever since Mom walked out, he's been my whole world.

Jordie must read the uncertainty in my expression when he looks up from his phone. "He really is, you know. Doctors aren't allowed to lie about these things."

He places a hand on my leg, running his thumb over my kneecap. My entire body warms at his touch, and I inhale deeply.

"I hope you're right. My dad and Faith are all I have."

Jordie nods. "I guess we have that in common—we both have one parent and an older sister."

I realize I never told Jordie the truth about my mom. But ever perceptive, he seems to read my mind and put two and two together.

"How old were you when your mom left?"

I draw in a deep breath and let it out slowly. I don't like to talk about my mother, mostly because I was so young when she left, I don't have any actual memories of her. For some reason, it makes me feel like an imposter for missing her so much, for being so angry about something I can't even remember.

But I am angry. And I'm hurt.

Growing up without her, without a mother's love . . . it stung. The Mother's Day tea party my school hosted every year was torture. Navigating my teen years without her guidance was so hard. My dad did his best, and I love him fiercely, but I was always acutely aware that something was missing.

With an inhale, I meet Jordie's eyes again. His expression is serious, concerned.

"I was two. Faith was six."

Jordie doesn't say anything else, he just pulls me close and hugs me. After a few minutes, I look up. Our eyes lock, and my stomach flip-flops.

"Thank you for today," I tell him. "For everything, really. I don't know what I would've done without you."

When he nods, I lean into him, our lips brushing so softly at first, I'm not sure it even counts as a kiss. But it's nice, whatever it is.

We search each other's eyes before kissing again, his arm slipping around my waist. Everything about the moment feels right—his hand on my knee, his lips against mine—like this is what we should always be doing. What we should have been doing from the moment we met.

"Your dad's going to be okay. You know that, right?" Jordie murmurs, his lips barely grazing my ear.

I lay my head on his chest, listening to the steady sound of his heartbeat and the soothing pattern of his chest rising and falling. Soon, my breath slows to match his rhythm.

"It's going to be okay," I whisper back, curling into him as he drapes his arm around my shoulders, my head fitting perfectly beneath his chin.

And for the first time all day, I actually believe it.

A little while later, as I start to nod off, Jordie gives my shoulder a squeeze and stands up, pulling me with him. He tilts my chin up with one finger and gives me a small smile.

"Looks like it's bedtime for you. Text me when you wake up in the morning. I'll drive you back to the hospital, okay?"

I nod, letting him wrap me in the warmest, safest hug ever.

CHAPTER THIRTEEN

No Guarantees

Jordie

God, this is awful.

I've never seen my teammate Asher like this. His eyes are wet with tears, and his broad shoulders shake with emotion as he leans against his fiancée, Bailey. She buries her face into his jacket as a single tear slips down her cheek.

There isn't a dry eye in the place.

Asher's eighty-seven-year-old grandmother, Lolli, passed away earlier this week. From what I understand, there wasn't a thing wrong with her— she just went to sleep one night and never woke up. Out of a show of support for one of my teammates, I'm sitting uncomfortably in a funeral home in San Diego. It's a quick trip with a twenty-four-hour turnaround time because of this week's game.

Most of the team is here, at least all the guys who are close with Asher. And I realize, for the first time, that I'm the only one here who's still single. Our goalie, Owen, is here with his wife, Becca, who's pregnant again, even though they have a one-year-old. Grant and Ana are here with their daughter. Justin and his fiancée, Elise, are here, as well as Teddy and his wife, Sara.

They say bad things happen in threes. First, Coach Allen's heart attack, and now there's been a death in the family for my teammate Asher. Basically, it has me on edge wondering what the hell else is going to go wrong.

After the service, which is actually really heartwarming and even funny at times, since several of her grandkids tell humorous stories about her, we all head back to Asher's grandmother's beach house. The humorous stories don't stop as we fill our plates full of the most delicious-looking Mexican food I've ever seen.

I hear several other colorful tales, including the one about the time Asher's grandmother set a record riding a mechanical bull at a local bar. Although, with each retelling of the story by Asher's sisters, and then by his cousins, the amount of time she lasted on that bull and the records she apparently set all get bigger and better. It's like a fishing story growing over time.

But I'm smiling, and the bourbon is flowing. Eventually, night falls, and we're all sitting outside in lawn chairs around a low-burning bonfire. The beach is deserted, except for our group, and the sound of the waves in the distance is calming. A light breeze ruffles the palm trees and flowering bushes at the edge of the sand.

"You okay, Ashe?" Grant, our team captain, asks.

Asher nods once, his gaze fixed on the fire. "Yeah. Just thinking."

His fiancée, Bailey, rubs his shoulder and gives him a sympathetic look.

"We wanted to get married before Lolli passed," Asher says, his voice thick with emotion. "Right here on this beach. Wanted to have her at our wedding, make sure she got to see us exchange our vows. But our careers got in the way, and now she's not going to be here for it."

Bailey gives him a sorrow-filled look. Between his schedule playing hockey and hers as a doctor, they're both busy. I really don't know much about their wedding planning, other than the fact that now it seems like waiting was a foolish idea.

I reach over to grip his shoulder. "I'm sorry for your loss." The words are generic, because I'm really not sure what to say, but I hope he knows I mean them.

He looks up to meet my eyes. "Don't wait, man. There are no guarantees in life."

I nod, feeling a little desperate and confused.

"The same goes for butt sex," a drunk Owen slurs. "Don't wait."

His wife elbows him the ribs while the rest of us chuckle.

"Come on." Bailey sniffs and straightens her shoulders. "Lolli wouldn't want us to cry for her. We should be smiling. Celebrating life. Making plans. Living it all to the fullest."

Asher nods, meeting her eyes. "You're right, babe."

"We should make this an annual tradition," someone suggests. "Pack up our bathing suits and come here every year. All of us."

"She'd like that," Bailey says with a sad smile.

"It's a deal. Next summer," Asher says. "Jordie, get yourself a date so you're not the odd man out, and put it on the calendar."

"Uh, sure," I mutter, suddenly feeling even more miserable. "Yeah, I'll see what I can do."

I gaze into the fire, lost in my thoughts. How the hell am I going to line up a date for a beach vacation when I can't even get the girl I like to go out to dinner with me?

Rising from my spot, I wander down the beach, out of earshot. I dial Harper's number, hoping to hear her voice, but she doesn't answer. I stare out at the dark water, wondering what I'm doing with my life.

• • •

The following week passes by in a blur.

After a couple of games in the Midwest, we're back for a series at home. And since we're back in Seattle, my thoughts naturally turn to Harper. I've been out of town a lot, first for the funeral and then playing hockey, but we've texted a couple of times.

My sister was right. When I was younger, it was easy to get girls. I had that rowdy teenage hockey-player charm, and I cranked it all the way up. Cocky, fun-loving, and—yeah, Harper hit it on the head—a little rough. Girls loved it. They practically fell into my arms. And then later, when I was older, they fell into my bed.

It never meant anything, and it never lasted. Which is why I'm still single, I guess. And now, out of the blue, I find myself wanting more, wanting something deeper and more serious then sex with a stranger.

But the only girl I want that with doesn't want a relationship with me. She's made that abundantly clear.

I think back a few weeks to when Harper's dad suffered a heart attack. She let me take her home and care for her. I ran her a bath, and fed her, and held her. And she let me without hesitation.

Yet I'm anything but certain she's changed her mind about hockey players. About *me*.

I guess there's only one thing to do.

Make her see how right we could be together.

• • •

I'm at practice a few days later, getting ready to take the ice again, when I see Harper unexpectedly approach the bench.

I tug off my helmet and wave her over. With a smile, she approaches.

"Hey, what are you doing here?" I ask.

"Just came by to drop off my dad's heart medication. He keeps forgetting to actually take the dang stuff."

"Gotcha."

I'm sweaty, and I'm sure my hair sticking up in like six different directions after pulling off my helmet. I probably smell too—best case, like deodorant; worst case, like sweat. But Harper doesn't seem to mind. She's grown up around hockey players, so none of this is new to her.

"Are you going to stay and watch the rest of the practice?" I ask, and she shakes her head.

"I can't. I'm working today."

Even though I need to be preparing for our drills, I'm not ready for her to go. I pull the book out of my bag that I've been reading since I tried to impress her with it at my faux book club.

"I'm on page two hundred thirty-six."

Her face lights up with a smile. "Oh, you're almost at my favorite part."

I'll admit, I'm more than a little curious about what that could be. "You wouldn't believe the amount of shit I got for reading this on the plane."

She laughs, an uninhibited, throaty sound that hits me square in the chest. "Well, I'm glad you're reading it. Still into the story?"

"Hell yeah. That part where he"—I lean closer, lowering my voice—"used a toy on her . . ."

Her eyes widen as they lift to mine. "Super hot, right?"

I smirk. "That would be fun to try sometime."

"It. Would." She swallows the words.

I chuckle, loving the way her cheeks turn pink.

Still holding the book in one hand, I flip to the page I left off on to show her. We're huddled close, and I know we must look like we're involved in an intimate discussion.

"Pussy-whipped," one of my teammates grumbles under his breath as he passes by us and takes the ice.

Teddy, probably. *Fucker*.

"Fuck off," I call out, never once taking my eyes off the gorgeous girl in front of me.

She's reduced to giggling and shaking her head.

"Anyway," I say, shoving the book back inside my bag, "I should be finished soon. I'm a slow reader."

"Well, I look forward to hearing your thoughts on the ending then." She grins.

"So, when are you going out with me again?"

Her lips twitch as she watches me. "I don't know. Are you asking me out again?"

"Would you say yes if I did?"

A couple more guys squeeze past us in full gear, which means I don't have much time left before I'm expected to be on the ice.

"Call me," she says coyly. "We can probably figure something out."

I still haven't fully processed what my sister told me about my interest in Harper—that I'm only into her because she's emotionally unavailable.

But something about seeing her today, here, on my turf, makes me want to be bold. It could also have something to do with the comment Asher made that night after the funeral. *Don't wait.*

"Good, because I've, um, had some time to

think since our last date . . ."

She smiles sweetly, gazing at me as she twists a lock of hair around her finger. "And?"

"I want a real shot with you. I'm done with casual. I want a girlfriend, Harper. I want that with you. What do you say?"

Her gaze falls to the floor between our feet, and my stomach drops. "I don't know, Jordie. I need some more time."

"Okay," I hear myself saying. My heartbeat thuds in my ears, and disappointment floods through me.

"I like you. I just . . . I never saw myself with a player. I had this whole plan, my own goals. I was ready to put myself and my life first."

I nod. "I get that. I do. And I know my schedule is tough."

Her mouth presses into a line, and an uncertain look passes across her features. "I can't just change everything at the drop of a hat."

Swallowing, I shove my hands into my gloves. "I didn't ask you to."

She gives me a pointed look. "And what if you

get traded to a team across the country?"

I don't have any answers, because on some level, I know she's right. Getting involved with me would mean her entire life would be dictated by a hockey schedule—the one thing she's waited years to be free from.

"I'll text you about that date." I tip my chin toward the ice. "I'd better get out there."

She nods. "Okay. I'll talk to you later."

God, why does this have to be so hard? It's like one step forward, two steps back, every time I see her.

The weird achy feeling in my chest doesn't go away as I skate toward where my team is huddled near the net. It doesn't go away as I watch Harper walk down the chute. And even when I make a huge play and score on Owen and get loud cheers from my teammates, it still lingers.

CHAPTER FOURTEEN

Not What They Seem

Harper

"Faith? Did you mean to leave your door unlocked?"

I push the front door to my sister's house open, craning my neck for signs of life. And, boy, do I find them. As I step gingerly into the entryway, I'm greeted by my sister's tasteful decor—complete with toys, scattered shoes, stuffed animals, colored pencils, and various articles of children's clothing scattered throughout. It's like a day-care center exploded in here.

"Hello?" I call out again. Down the hall, I can hear my niece Zoey babbling while the baby cries in one of the back rooms.

The TV is on, playing some educational cartoon I don't recognize at half volume, and I make my way to the kitchen. The path from the door to the granite-topped island is a minefield of stuffed animals and dolls that I would absolutely get in trouble with my niece for trampling. This I know from experience.

"Auntie Hopper!"

My four-year-old niece, Zoey, comes skidding around the corner, her tight, dark curls pulled into pigtails on either side of her head. She comes bounding up to me, wrapping her little arms around me.

I pick her up, shocked all over again by how big she's getting. It's only been a week since I saw her last, but I swear she's grown another two inches. "Hey, Zoey, you're getting so big! Where's your mommy?"

She points to the hall just as my tired, slightly frazzled-looking sister appears around the corner. Wearing stained yoga pants and an oversized sweatshirt, she carries a red-faced, tear-streaked Lila on her hip. I haven't seen her this way since Zoey was born.

"Baby Lila made a poo-poo," Zoey says in a nasally voice, pinching her nose and smiling at her use of potty language.

"Uh-oh, sounds like that was fun for Mommy," I say, giving Faith a sympathetic look.

"All part of the deal," she says with a weary smile, shifting Lila to her other hip and softly stroking her back. "I'm going to go put her down for a nap. Zo, you stay here with Auntie Harper, okay? Maybe you can show her some of your new crayons."

Zoey nods, straining for me to put her down. She barely tolerates being held now—she told me last time it's because she's a big girl. I set her feet on the floor and she takes off, grabbing my hand in hers, already giving me a mini-lecture on how much better her new box of crayons is than her old one.

Ten minutes later, Faith returns, stifling a yawn and smoothing a couple of flyaways along Zoey's hairline. "So, what do you need, Harp?" Faith doesn't look at me. Her eyes are still trained on the picture Zoey is drawing.

"I, uh, what? I just wanted to come by and say hi."

Faith tells Zoey to keep her crayon on the paper and off the table before giving me a skeptical look. "Harper, I love you, but you only come by for one of two reasons. Either you're here to complain about Dad, or you're here because there's something on your mind, and your friends didn't give you the answer you were hoping for."

I give her an incredulous look. "That is totally not true. I come to see my nieces and my sister."

She chuckles. "Okay, well, maybe so, but while you're here, we usually cover one of those two topics. So, which is it?"

Jeez, she's in a mood today.

I sigh and throw my hands in the air. "Okay, fine, you got me. I need your advice. But what makes you so sure that I already went to MK and Aurora? Can't a girl ask her big sister for some help?"

"I help baby Lila sometimes," Zoey says, pressing her lips together and excitedly pulling a purple crayon from the box.

Faith smiles and coos, "Hey, Zo, why don't you keep coloring, okay? Auntie Harper and I are going to sit on the couch right over there and have an adult conversation."

Zoey nods, and I follow my sister to the couch. With their open-concept kitchen, she still has a clear view of her daughter at the table and watches her closely, but we don't have to be so concerned about little ears.

"All right. Who's the guy?" she asks.

"What? No, I mean—"

She cuts me off. "Harper, we're on a time crunch here. I've only got half an hour before . . ." Her gaze shifts to Zoey she mouths, *that one goes down for a nap too*.

I sigh, pushing my fingers roughly through my hair. "He's a player."

"Oh?" Faith raises her eyebrows suggestively.

"On Dad's team."

"Oh." Her voice falls, her brows scrunching together.

"Right. Oh. And you know my whole thing about dating hockey players."

Her brow furrows even deeper. "What thing? I don't remember you having a thing."

"My thing! You know. God, you're going to make me explain it, aren't you?"

Faith looks at me expectantly, nodding her head

toward the giant clock on the wall.

"Ugh, fine. Ever since, you know, *our childhood*, I've made a pact with myself that I'd never date a hockey player."

"Oh, right. Because of all the . . ." She mouths the word *chlamydia*.

"Oh my God, what? No, you know that was just a one-time issue with that team Dad coached in the nineties."

Faith shrugs, gesturing for me to continue.

"I just . . . I got so sick of having to make sacrifices for the sake of hockey. Everything was always about the *team*. So I decided a while back that as an adult, I'd always put myself and my career first. No more uprooting my entire life for the sake of some brawny, stick-wielding, overconfident man-child."

But even as the words come out of my mouth, I'm not nearly as confident in them as I once was. And based on the look on my sister's face, she's not so sure about them either.

"Uh-huh. And is this guy a man-child?"

"Well, I mean, I think he used to be, but he's been pretty nice and mature, actually. He's not, you know, forcing me to do anything I don't want to do." I give Faith a pointed look, and she nods in understanding.

"What's his name?"

"Jordie."

Faith grabs her phone and begins typing something into Google. "Last name?"

I roll my eyes. "Prescott."

"Oh . . ." Faith's mouth lifts in a genuine smile.

I glance over her shoulder to see what she's looking at. The image of Jordie is a good one—captured at last year's Winter Classic, by the looks of the jersey he's wearing. He's not looking at the camera. Instead, his eyes are trained on something on the bench, and he's wearing a big, genuine smile. The dimple on his left cheek is so adorable, and his eyes are a fierce shade of blue. He's handsome in a boy-next-door kind of way. If that boy next door had an eight-pack.

"What a cutie. Six foot two. Two hundred pounds. *Damn*. A one-point-three-million dollar salary. He sounds like a catch."

"You're married, Faith," I remind her with an eye roll. "Surely, that doesn't, ya know, do anything for you."

Her eyes widen on mine. "Sweetie, I might be married, but if that did anything more for me, I might need to go rub one out in the bedroom real quick."

I shift uncomfortably while she continues scrolling through the online images of Jordie. "Faith, focus."

She sets down her phone, still smiling. "Fine. What did Dad say about this?"

I shrug. "He's cool with it. Apparently, he thinks pretty highly of Jordie."

"That's a good sign. I would trust Dad's opinion more than anything."

I nod. "But you know how it is. Growing up, everything revolved around hockey, and the constant change was miserable," I say, now trying to convince myself as much as my sister. "Like how we moved every two years to follow Dad's job, how we never had any real friends, how all we had was each other."

She stares blankly at me, then finally says with a shrug, "I don't know what you want me to say, Harp."

I give her a frustrated scoff. "I was hoping

you'd be supportive."

"Look around you," she says, her tone sharpening. "My life is changing diapers and managing my children's nap schedule. The most exciting thing that's happened this week is getting that new box of crayons at Target. Sure, it can be amazing, but at the end of the day, it's boring as heck a lot of the time. I miss all the different adventures we had as kids."

"I'm not sure *adventures* is the word I'd use."

I remember once in high school having to put my address on a job application, and I just blanked out. We'd moved three times that year, and not within the same city. We crossed state lines and time zones, heading to new and unfamiliar cities, often on short notice, packing up everything we owned to head to a place we'd never even visited before.

Eventually, I'd make some friends and unpack my bedroom, and just when things started to feel normal, everything would be uprooted again. It was all I knew, but that didn't mean I enjoyed it. I couldn't wait for when I was older and things could be different. All I wanted in the world was something stable. The comfort of something steady. To not blank out when someone asked me for my address.

Faith sighs and touches my hand. "Maybe not, but it's all about how you decide to see things. Harper, you know better than anyone what the reality of a hockey player's life is. Sure, you could be in a new place every other year. But who says you can't also pursue your career?"

"Well, I—"

"You work from home most of the week. All you need is a laptop and that brilliant mind of yours. You could figure it out. And besides, you're young. Think about how fun your life could be. It seems like you're stuck in thinking of what it was like as a kid, but you're not a kid anymore. You need to look at this as an adult. Think about it—new places, new restaurants, new friends. You'd have so many opportunities that might never present themselves to you otherwise, and you'd be doing it with someone who's all in with you."

"But . . . you love your life. You love being a mom."

She leans closer. "Of course I love being a mom. That's not what I'm saying. I'm just saying, hell, it might be nice to have more to look forward to in my life than trying a new Crock-Pot recipe."

I roll my eyes at her. "But what about Mom and Dad? His schedule was too much for their marriage."

The moment the words leave my mouth, I wish I could take them back. Faith and I have an unspoken agreement that we never talk about Mom. But Faith doesn't look upset. She just shakes her head.

"Mom and Dad had a lot of problems that had nothing to do with hockey."

My parents' marriage and subsequent divorce isn't a topic I want to venture into right now, so I just nod. "Maybe."

"Not maybe. Definitely," she mutters.

"Okay, fine. Say I do drop my life and follow him around the country, and then we get married, have kids, the works. I'd practically be a single mom. You saw how hard Dad had to work for us. And he didn't have all the extra training and shit that players do."

I know Faith's heard the saying, just like I did, that NHL stands for No Home Life. We used to joke about it.

"Oh, come on, you know that's not true. Players age out. By the time the two of you started thinking about settling down and having kids, he'd probably be ready to retire."

I stare at my sister in disbelief. I was so sure that she, of all people, would be on my side. She was right there beside me throughout our whole childhood. I thought that she would gush about how comforting and stable her new life is with her two kids, and her kind husband who won't get traded and move them across the country. But no. Apparently, her life now is *boring*.

"I don't even know what to say to you right now," I mumble, turning my attention to a small chip in my nail polish.

"Say that I'm right. Or at least that you'll re-think this whole *no dating a hockey player* thing. It might not be as bad as you think, and you could miss out on finding the love of your life, which would be an even bigger travesty than dating a hockey player."

I heave out a long sigh while Faith folds her legs underneath her. "I'll consider it."

"Also, if he's trying this hard to date you, it has to be serious to him. You're his coach's daugh-ter—he would never screw that up. If he breaks your heart, his hockey career would be over. Think about that."

I drop my gaze to my lap. It's possible she's right. Dad has the power to end his career if Jordie did me wrong.

"Okay, okay, I'll consider it."

"Good. Now tell me more about Jordie. The guy is seriously hot."

I chuckle, despite my conflicted mood, and decide that gossiping with my big sister outweighs stressing about what I should do.

"He's . . . yeah, he's hot." I can't deny that. "And a really good kisser." A smile twitches on my lips.

Her eyes widen, and her mouth lifts in a grin. "Why not just see where it goes, Harper? It could be the best thing to ever happen to you. I don't want you to miss out on something special with a seriously hot guy just because of your *no dating a hockey player* rule."

She pats my knee in a comforting way before standing up and telling Zoey it's time for her nap. Zoey whines in response, and Faith gives me a look that tells me to get out before the full-on meltdown begins.

After hugging them both good-bye, I walk quickly to my car in the chilly fall air, my mind spinning with my sister's unexpected take on things.

Could she really be right? Should I give Jordie a chance, even though being with him might end up meaning I need to uproot my whole life? I spend the whole drive home mulling over the different options in my head, but one thought sticks more than the rest.

Why not just see where this goes?

CHAPTER FIFTEEN

Losing Control

Jordie

I ran errands all afternoon, even stopping to get a couple's massage with Owen, which was every bit as strange as you might imagine. But, hey, we got a great deal. Afterward, I headed home to shower and shave, because tonight I finally have another date with Harper. After my shower, I quickly dressed in a pair of jeans, a button-down shirt, and a pair of boots.

Normally, I'd grab a condom before leaving the house for a date. Tonight, though? I'm all kinds of unsure about what to do. I want to be prepared, just in case, but I also don't want Harper to feel pressured or think that I expected sex to happen tonight. Because I definitely don't.

There's also the warning Tiffany gave me about

sex complicating things.

But that's not true, is it? Sex is the least compli-
cated thing ever. Except . . . when I picture getting
naked with Harper, I feel a lot more heart-pounding
anticipation than I ever have before.

Shit. I'm never this indecisive.

After a lot of hesitation, I shove a condom in
my pocket and take off.

When I stop in front of Harper's building, she's
already coming down the stairs, just like last time.
And just like before, the sight of her brings a smile
to my face.

I climb out of the truck and greet Harper, pulling her in for a hug. She brings her arms around
me and returns the hug with a smile. She smells
really good, like soap and light floral perfume, and
it doesn't escape my notice that she's dressed in
a skirt this time. I practically swallow my tongue
when I realize this, and thank the gods for my good
sense to pack a condom.

It doesn't mean anything will happen, dude.
But that doesn't stop my heart from pounding out
an uneven rhythm.

"You look amazing," I say, taking a step back

to release her.

Harper looks down, smoothing her black skirt over her thighs. She's wearing a matching black top, along with a bright pink coat and a pair of black ballet flats.

"You look nice too. Did you shave?" she asks, her lips tilting up in amusement.

I run one hand over my jaw. "I figured the occasion called for it."

I also manscaped, but I don't think now is the time to mention it.

She smiles. "Well, I'm honored."

Harper's been around hockey players long enough to know that we don't mess with our facial hair without good reason. Earning another date with this woman is a damn good reason.

Once she's secured in her seat, I maneuver the truck into traffic. "I hope you're hungry."

She nods. "Starved, actually. I spent the day at my sister's babysitting while she ran errands and went to the gym."

"That was nice of you."

Harper's lips tilt in a smile like she's daydreaming about something that happened today.

"How many nieces and nephews do you have?"

"Two nieces. Lily is six months and really sweet. Zoey is four and so naughty." She chuckles. "I don't know how my sister does it."

The mental image of Harper babysitting a couple of toddlers is pretty freaking cute. I wonder if she played make-believe with them and let them climb all over her.

At the restaurant, we leave my truck for the valet to deal with, and I escort Harper inside with my fingertips resting on the small of her back. By the time we're seated at a quiet table in the back, the air between us feels thick with chemistry and something electric.

I'm captivated by the smallest things, like the way she crosses her legs and places the napkin across her bare knees, and the way she leans forward and meets my eyes when I ask about her family.

During dinner, she fills me in on the antics of her nieces while we feast on Chinese food, sharing honey sesame chicken, broccoli, and steaming bowls of egg flower soup.

"How are you getting along with the guys on the team?" she asks. "This is your second season, right?"

I nod. "Yeah, and it's been great. It was tough at first, but I'm adjusting. There are a lot of big personalities. And most of the guys have been doing this a lot longer than me, so it's a lot of just shutting my mouth and paying attention."

She smirks. "That can't be easy for you. You're pretty mouthy."

I lean close and touch her hand, lacing her fingers between mine. "When I want something, I go after it."

"And what do you want?" She gives me a heated look, and I feel my cock twitch.

Down, boy.

"All I want is a fair shot with you. I like you, Harper, and I'm all in."

"I gotta say . . ." She smiles, leaning closer. "You surprised me, Jordie."

"How so?"

She shrugs. "Well, I kind of expected you to be a macho, douchey bro type. But you're not. Not really."

I chuckle, rubbing my thumb over the back of her hand. "Thanks. I think."

I think what she's saying is she didn't want to like me, but she does. I guess I'm growing on her—like a fungus. At this point, I'll take it.

I pay our bill while Harper sips on her second glass of white wine. I limited myself to one beer since I'm driving. Harper gave me a surprised look when I said this, and it made me wonder what kind of guys she's gone out with in the past. I would never put her in any danger, no matter how small the risk.

"So . . ." Harper grins, setting down her now-empty wineglass. "Did you finish the book?"

I chuckle and lean in close. "I did."

She lifts her eyebrows playfully. "And . . ."

"And I already bought the second book in the series. Does that answer your question?"

She grins. "I love that so much. But I own it . . . I could have loaned it to you."

Leaning back, I cross my arms over my chest. "It's all good."

"Are you going to tell me what you thought about the ending?" Her eyes hold a challenge.

"It was hot and sweet, and honestly . . ." I hesitate and shake my head.

"What? Tell me." There's a slight flush to her cheeks.

"I read it twice, that part where he . . ." I push my tongue into the side of my cheek and meet her eyes.

"Oh yeah. That was delicious." She's slightly breathless as she says this.

The scene was hot as fuck, and I decide *delicious* is as good a way as any to describe it.

"Someone should write a romance novel about a hockey player," I say next.

This gets a big laugh out of Harper. Only I wasn't kidding.

"It could be a whole series. One book about the player who falls for his coach's daughter . . ." I wink at her.

"Another about a player who falls for a teammate's sister," she says.

I frown, shaking my head. "No way. Everyone

knows sisters are off-limits."

Her gaze moves to my lips and lingers there. It's impossible not to notice, and sends a bolt of heat racing down my spine.

"If you're ready to get out of here, I noticed an ice cream shop a couple doors down."

She nods. "That sounds perfect."

This date is going even better than I imagined it would.

While the valet goes to retrieve my truck, we hop in line next door at a place called Wanna Spoon? Agreeing it's the best name for an ice cream shop we've ever heard, we each get a small ice cream cone.

Watching Harper lick rum-flavored tres leches ice cream from the top of her cone gives me all kinds of dirty ideas about how we can spend the rest of the evening. But I force a deep breath into my lungs and try to pretend like this condom isn't burning a hole in my pocket.

We hop into my truck and polish off our dessert as I make the drive back to her place.

Harper directs me to pull off the road and park in the nearly empty lot behind her building. I do, noticing how dark and deserted it is back here. One streetlight faintly illuminates the lot. We're alone, for the first time all night.

I turn to face her. "I guess this is it. Unless you want to invite me in . . ." I flash her a mischievous smile.

Her mouth lifts in a smirk, even as a determined look overtakes her face. "It's only our second official date. Which means no sex tonight."

"Of course not. I'm a gentleman. We definitely won't be having any sex."

She smiles, shooting me a coy look that says she can tell I'm full of shit.

I love it.

And she's right—I want to press her against the first solid surface we can find and nail her so hard. But I won't. Not unless she asks very, *very* nicely.

Leaning in, I slide one hand into the hair at the back of her neck and draw her closer. She meets me halfway and presses her mouth to mine.

The kiss starts off slow and sweet—until I make a low growling sound in the back of my throat. Then Harper's lips part, and she tangles her tongue with mine in hot, confident strokes. She tastes like rum and sugar, and I can't get enough.

I'm ravenous for her.

I never really saw the point of kissing before. Yes, I've kissed a lot of girls, but it was always because it was expected. Something to get me from point A to point B, a box to check off on the foreplay list so we could move on to something better. But with Harper, kissing *is* the main event. It's that good.

Tearing my mouth from hers, I bring my lips to her neck, nipping and sucking at the tender skin of her throat. She smells like sugar and lavender, and I want to devour her. Harper is all too happy to let me. Her hands move from my chest to my biceps, and then finally push into my hair. She makes incoherent sounds that I'm quickly falling in love with.

I pull back just a fraction to measure her reaction, knowing that dazed look on Harper's face is all for me. And I fucking love it.

When she opens her eyes, they're stormy and conflicted. "Maybe you shouldn't come inside," she says, catching her plump lower lip between her teeth.

I tuck some loose strands of her hair behind her ear. "I can keep my hands to myself."

"I know. But maybe I can't."

Fuck.

I touch her lower lip with my thumb. "Are your panties wet, Harper?"

She makes a little choked breathless sound. "Jordie."

I caress her cheek with my thumb. "It's after midnight. And we got ice cream. So technically, this is another date. Our seventh now."

She gives me a sassy look. "Seventh? How are you calculating these so-called dates?"

"Well, the night we met was one," I say cautiously.

"You're counting the charity auction?"

"The auction so counts," I say firmly. "The animal shelter was two. The book club was three." I tick these off on her fingers, pressing my lips to each one.

She laughs, but I'm not deterred.

"The night your car broke down and we had dinner at my place was four."

She gives me a skeptical look.

"Ice skating was date number five. And the dinner tonight was six."

"So?" She meets my gaze with a wide-eyed look.

"So . . ." I touch my lips to her neck. "I'm saying it was too soon to have sex on our sixth date, but maybe it's not anymore."

"Oh." She licks her lips, still watching me with a hot, hungry expression. "You make a pretty convincing argument."

I expected her to laugh and tell me to shut up. What I didn't expect was for her to crawl across the center console and into my lap, but that's exactly what she does.

Her skirt has ridden up her parted thighs until she's pressing her center right into me. It's the best kind of torture. Anything resembling control on my part is gone.

Her hot mouth fastens to mine again, and my hands are suddenly full of her ass as she grinds her lower half against mine.

The sound that pushes past my parted lips is rough. A little helpless.

I want this so badly. I'm not used to these feelings. The desperate, urgent need for her—the desire to hold her in my arms and make her come—it's all-consuming. Blinding. But I don't want to screw this up.

I rest my forehead against hers and take a deep breath. *Slow down, Jordie.*

I don't want to rush through this like some horny teenager. I want Harper to know she's important to me, that this moment means something to me, and I don't want it to be a one-time thing. If I race through this, I'm scared she'll think she's nothing more than a quick fuck.

But then she grinds that soft, luscious ass over me again, and I swallow a whimper.

When I reach beneath her shirt and cup her breast, she softens against me. And when I pinch her nipple, she moans.

Pushing her jacket down off her shoulders, I strip it off her. I notice her feet are bare, and see her ballet flats on the floorboard on the passenger side.

"Fuck, Harper," I murmur.

"What?" she says breathlessly against my lips.

"I can't keep my hands off you."

"Then don't."

Pushing up the front of her shirt, I tug down her bra, and immediately have my mouth full of her perfect tits. Harper shifts restlessly in my lap, and I rasp out a groan.

While I suck on one perky nipple and then the other, Harper's hands explore, halfway unbuttoning my shirt so she can run her palms over my chest and abs.

"Look at me." My voice comes out as a grumbled command, and those beautiful dark eyes return to mine. "You're sexy as hell, and I want this so much . . . but I won't do anything you're not ready for. So, just say the word and everything stops."

"Jordie, stop talking," she murmurs, her voice low.

Fuck.

"I can do that," I whisper, dragging my palms across the weight of her breasts again.

She arches into me and lets out a breathless sound. I could worship her breasts all night, but I sense Harper wants my hands somewhere else.

When I touch the front of her panties, her answering moan is soft and so delicious. Pushing my fingers under the elastic, I'm rewarded with another incoherent sound.

"Unzip me," I say on a groan, my lips traveling from her mouth to her neck.

She works to free my aching cock, wrapping it in her fist to stroke me as I push my jeans down over my hips. I draw a fortifying breath. It feels so fucking good. So much better than my own hand—which has been my only companion since I met her.

"Oh." Harper makes a breathless sound as she gazes down between us at my thick cock.

I have a big dick. It's not bragging . . . it's just the truth.

"Jordie, *holy shit*."

A prideful noise rumbles in my chest as Harper slides her hand up and down my swollen shaft. *Damn, that feels good.* She strokes me with just the right amount of pressure and speed.

Things are spiraling out of control fast, but I'm unable to stop it, especially when Harper's thumb rubs over the head of my cock, capturing the moisture leaking from the tip.

I squeeze her breasts and suck at the hot skin

on her neck. She moans and rocks her hips closer. Jesus, I can't take much more of that.

"Condom. Left pocket." My voice trembles with need.

With her teeth buried in her plump lower lip, Harper digs the condom from my pocket and with zero hesitation, rips it open.

I swallow and pull a deep breath into my lungs. "You want to . . . put that on me?" I ask between gasps.

Her slender fingers roll the condom down over me, and I almost die from happiness on the spot. Then Harper lifts up on her knees and presses her mouth to mine. When her tongue enters my mouth, I moan.

The way she shifts her panties to the side and sinks down on me almost makes me want to get down on one knee and propose. Because *damn*. There's just something about a confident woman who takes what she wants.

I let out a tight breath and shift my hips up, placing one hand on her ass for leverage. Harper keeps on lowering herself until I'm fully buried inside her. We both let out a heavy groan.

The realization that Harper doesn't do things like this—that she's as overcome by desire as I am, and the fact that she threw her rules out the window—it lights me up inside like a goddamn Christmas tree.

The caveman inside me wants to pound his chest, but the urgent need to fill her with my cock wins out. And so I do—in long, deep thrusts that send heat and pleasure through every nerve ending in my body. She's incredible. Tight and hot, and *wow*.

"Fuck. *Fuck*, wait. I need a minute." I grunt, giving my hips a slow, experimental thrust.

Harper digs her nails into my shoulders, and her head drops forward onto my shoulder. "Don't stop, please." She doesn't wait—she begins riding me, sliding up and down, and gripping me with her inner muscles on each slow pass.

Her breathless gasps and little moans are ruining me. I grip her hips and take control, thrusting up each time she pushes down.

Her uneven heartbeat pounds against my chest, and her body trembles as she rides me. This moment is so much better than I ever imagined sex with Harper would be—and believe me, I've imagined it a lot.

Would I have preferred we be in a bed where I could lay her out and explore every inch of her naked body? Of course. But there's something really fucking satisfying about this too. I can't see her body, but I can feel all her primal responses to me. Her warm, flushed skin, the wet heat between her legs. It's almost more intimate somehow.

"Jordie, more," she says on a groan, bouncing harder in my lap.

Oh. Fuck.

Dead kittens. Calculus. Hot garbage.

It doesn't work. I'm too far gone for this girl, and she's hot and responsive in my arms. She feels incredible around me, almost uncomfortably tight in all the best ways.

"I need to slow down. I'm about to come," I say, breathless.

"Then come." She sounds equally as out of breath.

"No fucking way. Gotta get you there first, babe." I reach down and touch her clit, circling it with my thumb.

Harper shudders against me, and her pussy tightens around my cock. "Come, Jordie." She breathes out the words. "And then I'll come on your tongue."

Fuck. Hearing those dirty words leave her mouth is my undoing. Plus, well, that's just a really tempting offer. Because Harper riding my face until she loses control? It's the hottest thought ever.

"Baby. Fuck. *Fuck.* You feel so good on my cock."

I press my face into her neck, and seconds later, it's all over. I come hard, gripping her ass in one hand, and burying the other beneath the curtain of her dark hair.

"Yes, Jordie." She groans, tightening her inner muscles as I empty myself into the condom.

I've barely recovered before Harper attempts to climb off. Simultaneously reclining my seat, I tug her up my body until her pussy is in my face. I press a soft kiss to her silken flesh, then dive in for a real taste. *Damn, that's good.*

"Oh . . ." She moans softly, her thighs quivering. "Fuck."

Groaning, I bury my tongue inside her. "You

taste so sweet."

With a shocked yelp, Harper flattens her palms on the headrest by my head. I suck hard, feeling her tremble as my lips and tongue tease her clit. When I sink two fingers deep inside and curl them up, she jolts against me, and I smile.

"There?" I whisper against her flesh.

She whimpers. "Oh . . . wow. Yeah. *Uh . . .*"

I love that she's reduced to one-syllable words. Smiling, I devour her like I can't get enough. And truth be told, I can't.

Another stroke inside her, and Harper gasps, her body clamping down on my fingers as she comes apart. I kiss and suck as her hips shift restlessly against me, making sure she rides out every last wave of pleasure.

When she's thoroughly satisfied, I pull her down, settling her in my lap again. She curls into my chest, tucking her face against my neck.

After a few shaky breaths, Harper moves back to the passenger side. "So, that just happened," she says, burying her face in her hands.

Chuckling, I pull her close. Well, as close as possible with the center console in our way. "That was fucking awesome."

Her eyes meet mine, and a soft smile brightens her face.

"Best seventh date I've ever been on. Hands down."

She smirks. "Same."

"I want to cuddle." I give her a soft look. "But I, uh, also need to deal with this condom."

"Is that your way of getting out of after-sex cuddling?" she says, laughing at me.

It's the best sound ever. Because, *holy shit*, I still can't believe Harper just let me fuck her. In my truck. It was hot and amazing and perfect, and I can't wait to do that again. As soon as humanly possible. Which is, give or take, like twenty minutes.

I smirk. "I actually love cuddling. I mean, what's not to love?"

She rolls her eyes, adjusting the hem of her skirt. "You want to come inside?"

"I'd love to."

I remove the latex and wad it into a napkin, then fasten my pants and follow Harper into her apartment to continue what is turning out to be the best date of my entire life.

CHAPTER SIXTEEN

Hello, Heaven? It's Me, Harper

Harper

Waking up next to Jordie is pure, unadulterated heaven.

The weight of his thick arm thrown across my chest? *Heaven.* His lean, hard body pressing against my backside? *Heaven.* His cuddling game? *Absolute freaking heaven.*

I savor the first few moments when I wake up before him, slowly and carefully turning over so I can look at him without disturbing his blissful slumber. Jordie is so cute when he's sleeping, and the peaceful look on his face is only made more attractive by how warm and safe I feel lying here next to him, surrounded by all this warm, bulky muscle.

Last night was . . . I don't think I even have the

words to describe it. Incredible? Mind-blowing? The best sex of my life? Any word I can think of is putting it too lightly.

I thought I was ready to take it slow, to wait and see if I was sure about him. But last night, something just clicked into place. Jordie is tall and broad and delicious. And he read my favorite romance novel. He didn't have to, but he did. And then discussed it with me. I liked that a lot. And our dinner date was perfect. It turns out, when I want something, I go after it. And I have zero regrets about what happened between us last night.

I run a finger lightly along his face, tracing the hint of stubble on his defined jaw.

His eyes flutter open, and the smile that spreads across his face is sweet. Happy. It does funny things to my stomach.

"Good morning," he says, more a hungry growl than a greeting.

We had sex again last night before falling asleep, and it was perfect. Slower. Less frantic. But every bit as hot. I guess I threw my own rules about not having sex on our date out the window. Once wasn't enough. And now, waking up beside him, I'm not even sure twice was either.

"Good morning," I say as he pulls me tighter to him, his mouth pressing against the space between my neck and my shoulder.

Okay, I'm definitely awake. And judging by the stirring against my thigh, so is he.

The kiss starts out slow and lingering, but just like last night, all at once, Jordie shifts us into the next gear. He nips at my lower lip, his hands wandering over my body. One cradles my face while the other finds my ass, squeezing and moving dangerously close to my center.

I grind against him, and he groans, kissing the skin along my jaw, forcing a low sound from my throat.

"I like waking up next to you," he says softly against my skin.

"Me too."

When we went out last night, I didn't intend for him to stay over. But after I was able to quiet the insecure voice inside my head and operate on instinct, I invited him inside. And once he was here in my space, being affectionate, kissing me, laughing at the family photos back from when my dad had hair . . . I didn't want Jordie to go.

I drag my fingers along his skin, pushing the sheet farther down his hips. Heat and desire bloom inside me.

While my fingertips explore, Jordie's lips tilt up in a smirk. "You like teasing me?"

I can only grin. Maybe my resistance to hockey players has been my worst decision to date. Because after this . . . *holy cow*.

How could I ever go back to dating a mere mortal? Stanley in IT that I dated last year is a distant, sad memory.

Because Jordie naked?

Is . . . holy fucking shit.

He's big all over. A broad, sculpted chest. Defined abdominal muscles. Hard, strong thighs. His proud erection is both thick and long, and I can't wait to get my *everything* all over it. Mouth. Hands. Vagina. They're all scrambling for a turn. Thankfully, I have enough sense not to open my mouth and blurt this to him.

"Come here," he whispers, tugging me even closer. His big, calloused hands roam over my heated skin, lingering on my breasts, stroking between my legs. When he feels how wet I am, he grunts in approval. Potent satisfaction races through me.

When I wrap him in my fist, Jordie tilts his hips forward, sliding into my hand and rewarding me with a low, pleased sound.

"You're gonna kill me, sweetheart," he rumbles.

"Well, we can't have that." I smirk at him.

Sex has never been like this before. This intense. This pleasure-filled. This perfect.

Normally there's a probation period—a learning of each other's bodies and anticipating each other's next moves. But with Jordie, there's none of that. There's only pure instinct and blinding pleasure. He's like a meal I want to devour.

His soft, sure touches bring me closer to the edge, but my body aches for more. I make a breathy noise, and Jordie's hooded gaze meets mine with a look of adoration.

"That feel good, baby?" His voice is husky and laced with sex.

Which actually gives me a pretty good idea.

I roll over onto my back and pull a condom out of a drawer in the bedside table. His hand settles at my waist, and he gives it a light squeeze.

"You're not sore from last night?" he asks with a hint of concern.

It's a valid question. This will be our third time having sex in twelve hours, but the answer is no. Pushing my pelvis into his, I give him a heated look.

Jordie's mouth covers mine in a tender kiss, his tongue hot and seeking when I part my lips. And while his deep kisses send heat fracturing down my spine, I eagerly roll the condom down his length.

We're lying side by side, my knees parted to accommodate his big body against mine. Using one hand to grip my hip and the other to align himself, he joins us with a confident stroke. I gasp and clutch his muscular ass.

With shallow, halting breaths, Jordie finds the perfect rhythm. And when I reach between us to touch myself, he groans loudly.

"Love watching you. That's so hot."

I wrap one leg around his waist and place my palm against his stubbled jawline, turning his face to mine to steal another kiss. He feels so good, the muscles between my legs twitch, and I draw a fortifying breath.

"I'm gonna—" But a moan swallows the rest of the sentence.

"Me too." He grunts, and we come together, my body shuddering around him.

I'm breathless and dizzy. He is so, *so* good at that.

Jordie carefully withdraws and removes the condom. After it's been taken care of, he rejoins me on the bed. When he draws me close, my heart is still hammering against my ribs.

"You're amazing," he mumbles into my neck, his lips trailing along my skin.

I smile and nestle closer into his broad chest. As good as it feels to lie here and cuddle with him, I know we can't stay in bed forever.

"Breakfast?" I ask, slipping out of bed to gather a pair of underwear and jeans from my dresser.

"I have time for a bite," he says, appearing behind me and placing his lips on my shoulder.

"Keep that up, and we'll never make it out of this room." My stomach growls at the same time that something below it aches for more.

He groans. "Fine," he says gruffly, pulling on his jeans and stretching a T-shirt over his broad shoulders.

I could watch this man get dressed every day for the rest of my life. It's my second favorite thing after undressing him.

I slip into a comfy sweater, grab my purse and coat, and we head out. A waffle bar is only a couple of blocks from my place, and the short walk gives us a chance for prolonged snuggling. Jordie wraps an arm around me, and I bury myself in the warm space between his arm and his side. I love being with him like this. He makes me feel so safe and chosen and special.

When we arrive at the periwinkle-blue little A-frame, Jordie gives me a hesitant look.

"Just trust me," I say, and he shrugs, opening the door and shuffling in behind me.

We're instantly met by the delicious smell of maple syrup, vanilla, and warm, made-from-scratch waffles. The inside of the shop is equally as colorful, the tables and chairs inside all painted in pastel colors. Once we're seated, we're handed mint-green menus, chock-full of various waffle flavors, each one wilder than the last.

"How have I never heard of this place?" Jordie says, his eyes widening as the table next to us is served their food.

Each plate is stacked three waffles high, some topped with the usual things like whipped cream, syrup, blueberries, chocolate chips, or bananas. Others have more daring toppings like bacon, fried chicken, grilled onions, or mac and cheese. One even looked like it might have some kind of chili pepper on it.

"Clearly, you're not following the same Instagram accounts as me." I grin, my stomach growling even louder this time.

As I giggle and Jordie laughs, we survey the menu, trying to decide what we want to order. Eventually, I settle on the cinnamon roll waffles, and he chooses the "world's best chicken and waffles," and we both promise to share. I take a sip of my coffee, which I don't feel like I need so desperately after the wake-up call I was lucky enough to receive less than an hour ago.

Out of nowhere, Jordie laughs, and I give him a quizzical look.

"Do I have something on my face?" I'll think twice next time I order a latte with extra foam.

"No," he says, taking my hand in his, a broad smile on his face. "I just can't believe how incredible you are. Look at me. I can't stop smiling."

My heart melts into a puddle on the spot. "You're not so bad yourself."

If you'd have told me a month ago that I'd be sitting in the world's cutest waffle shop with Jordan freaking Prescott, a rookie on my dad's hockey team, smiling from ear to ear and feeling like I've just won the dating lottery, I'd have told you to check what you're smoking. But here I am, and here he is. And I can't imagine being anywhere else.

As we eat dig into our waffles, we chat about the usual things. Our jobs, our busy schedules, what movies we're dying to see. I've just about lost track of time when the waitress comes by to give us the check, and Jordie takes a hasty glance at his phone.

"Shit," he says, his face falling.

"What's wrong?" My mind immediately goes to the worst. My dad. One of his teammates. Someone could be really hurt.

"Nothing," he says, pulling his lips into a thin, taut line. "Except that I have to leave soon. I forgot

I'd made plans with a couple of my teammates for this morning."

"Sounds fun," I say, but I can't ignore the slight sinking feeling. Everything about this date has been perfect, and I don't want it to end.

But I'm also an adult, and I know that I can't just steal Jordie away and lock him in my bedroom for three days. Although I do make a mental note to bring up that scenario at a later date.

Besides, what's that saying? Distance makes the heart grow fonder, or whatever?

"Eh, we'll see. We'll probably spend most of the time talking team business."

He settles the bill, despite my protest, and I have to admit that it's sweet. Who doesn't like being a little old-fashioned every once in a while?

Besides, I can't pretend anymore that we aren't actually dating. This is real. It's happening. And despite all my earlier reservations, I want to be here, to see this through. Wherever it might take me.

When we step outside, the autumn breeze is a little chillier than it was before. Jordie wraps me up in his arms, and we make the short trek back to my apartment door.

"I should probably head out. They'll never let me live it down if I'm late again. Especially because of a girl."

"Oh, so I'm just some girl now?" I arch a playful brow at him.

With his hands on my hips, he pulls me in for a kiss. It's long and slow and sweet, the kind of kiss that warms me straight down to my toes.

"Not just any girl. You're my girl," he says. And once again, I'm lost in those clear blue eyes.

"Thanks for walking me home."

He brushes a stray hair from my forehead and tucks it behind my ear, and I have to keep myself from actually swooning.

"I'll call you," he says, kissing me one more time before walking down the few steps and making his way to his truck.

I watch him leave, the warmth from our kiss still lingering in every inch of my body.

All those worries I had about Jordie before? They're long gone by this point. I've tossed them out the window. I can't believe how scared I was, how sure I was that Jordie wasn't right for me.

And for once in my life, I'm happy that I was wrong.

CHAPTER SEVENTEEN

Times Are Changing

Jordie

C all me after the team dinner tonight, Harper's text says.

My teammates and I are on a quick overnight trip to Vancouver. As soon as I make it back to the hotel room I share with Grant after the team dinner, I press her contact info in my phone.

Settling onto the plush bed, I wait impatiently for the phone to ring. When she answers, my mouth lifts in a lazy smile. "Hey."

She laughs, the sound musical and light. "Hey."

"What are you doing?"

"Just sitting on my bed with my notebook. I'm making some notes for the article I need to write tomorrow." I can hear her shift against the mattress.

"Nice. What's it about?"

"This one is just a boring tech article."

I nod. "Gotcha."

Now that I know her goal of writing a book someday, I've been encouraging Harper with her writing, but I also don't want to be annoying about it. The last time we talked about it, we were lying in her bed. I'd never stayed the whole night with a woman before. Yes, I've had a lot of sex, but having pillow talk is new for me and different. I liked hearing her talk about her goals while we laid there naked.

I remember that next morning. I was in no hurry to leave. Waking up with a warm, sleepy Harper, her soft curves molded to my chest, the tantalizing press of her ass to my groin. I didn't want to ever want to move from that spot.

"What are you up to?" she asks.

"We just got back from dinner."

"Where'd you go?"

"Some Thai place. Teddy made the reservation. He's basically a foodie, always wanting to try the newest restaurants in the cities we travel to. Last month, we went to some pop-up restaurant by a chef in Phoenix."

"That sounds cool." After a pause, she drops her voice lower when she asks, "Are you alone?"

A sizzle of heat bolts down my spine. I glance across the room to where Grant sits on his bed with his laptop, sipping on an electrolyte solution.

"Uh, no. Grant's here," I say.

His gaze drifts from his laptop over to mine, and he gives me a curious look.

It's Harper, I mouth silently.

"Can you get some privacy?" Harper murmurs. "I wanted to tell you all about how much I've missed you."

Which is basically a chill way of saying *I want to talk dirty with you*. I have no idea what's come over her, but I'm completely on board with it.

As my body reacts to the idea of phone sex, I clear my throat and give Grant a pleading look. "Any chance you're going out tonight?"

Grant's brows rise almost to his hairline. "What the hell, man?" He never goes out, and I've been rooming with him long enough to know this.

I shrug, acting casual, but I'm sure there's a

desperate look in my eyes.

"I'm not leaving the room so you two can have phone sex, FYI." His tone is unamused.

As I consider begging, he shakes his head and goes back to whatever it is that has captured his attention on the screen. Most likely, he's watching video of his shifts against Vancouver, studying his performance for weakness. That's just the kind of player Grant is. Dedicated. Loyal. Always striving to do better, to be more, both at home and on the ice.

Sharing so many hotel rooms, I've learned a lot about him. First, Grant is very meticulous when we travel. He unpacks when we first arrive, always hanging his suit in the closet so it doesn't wrinkle, lining up his shoes neatly on his side of the room. He keeps his toiletries in a bag on the counter, versus scattered all over the bathroom like I'm prone to doing. Only now he's not just a meticulous roommate, he's also a massive cock-block.

I rub at a spot on my left thigh, the bruise purple and tender from a blocked shot a few days ago.

"My asshole of a roomie won't leave," I mutter, firing an annoyed look at Grant, who gives me the finger in reply. "I'll be back tomorrow night after the game, though. It'll be late, but will you come over?"

"What time?" she asks breathlessly.

"Around midnight."

I hold my breath, positive she's about to shoot me down and say it's too late. Sometimes my game schedule really fucking sucks.

"I don't have to go into work the following day until eleven for a meeting with my editor."

Hope blooms in my chest. "So you'll come?"

I can hear the smile in her voice when she responds. "I could definitely do that."

I'm smiling when I say, "I'll see you tomorrow night."

• • •

After arriving home, I've only just rolled my suitcase into my closet and slipped off my shoes when my building intercom announces a visitor.

She's here.

My heart trips over itself in an effort to speed up, and as I race to the front door, I loosen my tie.

It was thoughts of being alone with Harper again that carried me through the final period of tonight's game. And now that I'm about to get that opportunity, I'm equal parts nervous and filled with excitement. I'm so far gone for this girl, it's not even funny.

When I open the door, Harper's eyes light up with a smile. *God, she's beautiful.*

"Come here. I fucking missed you."

With her mouth lifted in a curious smile, she steps across the threshold until she reaches me. Standing before me in her flats, Harper barely clears my chin.

I touch her cheek and lift her lips to mine. Her mouth is warm, and she tastes like mint. My heart pounds out an uneven rhythm as we kiss by the door.

I'm not used to catching feels. The girls I've been with in the past weren't interested in my heart. They only wanted the organ below my belt, which I was happy to supply. Now, though? Things are changing, and I don't hate it.

Something is changing for Harper too. I can feel it. Every kiss is saturated with emotion. Hot and unyielding.

After a few more slow kisses, I pull back and meet her eyes. "Did you watch the game?"

She nods. "I didn't so much as watch the *game* as I watched *you*. Every time you took the ice, I was on the edge of my seat."

I love the idea of that, that my shifts were the only thing that held her interest in an otherwise energetic and fast-paced game.

"What?" I ask when her lips quirk against mine.

She presses her hands flat against my chest, pushing aside the lapels of my jacket. "You in this suit is giving me all kinds of ideas."

"Oh yeah?" I smirk. "What kind of ideas?"

Her manicured hand curls around my tie, and she tugs. "Is your bedroom down here?"

She tips her chin toward the hall. I nod, my mouth suddenly dry.

Last time we were together, we spent the night at her place. And while she's been here once before, we didn't venture into my room.

Once inside my bedroom, Harper pauses and looks around, taking in the king-size bed that I didn't bother to make before I left, so it's messy with a navy-blue duvet flung haphazardly over it. My dresser is cluttered with a couple of old receipts and some loose change. A dead potted plant my sister gave me last year sits on a stack of books.

My decorating may leave a lot to be desired, but Harper doesn't comment on my bare bedroom. Her eyes find mine again, and she smiles and takes a step toward me. I kiss her lips, her cheeks, her neck.

Her hands wander and begin working at the buttons on my dress shirt, then tug at the buckle on my belt. My dick is fully hard now as I make quick work of Harper's sweater and leggings until she's standing beside my bed in her underwear.

"As much as I like your suit, I think I'm going to like it even better on the floor."

It's a thousand-dollar suit, and I've never been so careless as to leave it on the floor, but that's exactly what happens when I strip it off. When I shrug off my shirt, Harper sucks in a sharp inhale.

Her gaze tracks lower, over my torso, and zeroes in on some brutal-looking welts and bruises. When she leans down to give them a gentle kiss, I hiss out a breath, and she meets my eyes with a concerned look.

"Does it hurt?"

"Not as much now that you're here."

Her gaze softens. "I'll kiss it all better."

The line is cheesy, but I love it.

Slowly sinking to her knees on the carpet between my feet, Harper kisses each and every bruise and mark along my ribs. Her mouth moves lower, and my knees tremble. When the heat of her mouth presses over my straining erection, I tug down my briefs, and before I can even gather a breath into my lungs, her mouth is all over my cock. Hot and wet and demanding.

"*Fuck.*" I groan, burying my hand in her hair.

She doesn't so much as go down on me as much as she *devours* me. Consumes me. It's hot as hell.

You know how some girls give a pretty blow job? Their eyes meet yours, their lashes fluttering, their tongue lightly tracing to make it look cute and sorta graceful? Well, Harper's nothing like that.

Her eyes are closed in concentration, and her brow is creased. She makes little gasping sounds, and her hand is wet with spit as she works my cock with it while her mouth does wicked, filthy things to me. With her other hand, she reaches below to massage my balls, and my eyes almost roll back in my head.

Fuck yeah, she's a multitasker.

"Hmm?" She groans, looking up at me.

Shit. Did I say that out loud?

"Nothing. It feels so *fucking* good," I grunt out.

Harper only smiles.

She has me feeling all kinds of things. Aroused and excited, and *fuck* . . . just desperate.

Pleasure rockets through me. It's so good, I almost can't stand it. With one slow worshipful lick after another until I'm reduced to grunts and monosyllables, she goes at me hard, eager for everything, and I'm here for it.

Her mouth moves lower, finding my balls, and my thighs tremble. She sucks one ball into her mouth, and I let out a guttural sound, my back arching involuntarily. *Damn, that feels good.*

"Fuck. Your mouth is perfect, baby."

Harper sucks hard, gasping for breath. The fact that she wants my cock more than she wants air? Huge fucking turn-on.

"Shit . . . *yeah, like that*," I say on a groan. "Fuck, I'm going to come."

My thighs tense. Too late to pull back now. I come hard, groaning out Harper's name as she swallows me, taking everything I give her.

"That was so hot," she says, pressing a kiss to my abs and looking up at me with an appraising expression.

"Get up here." I'm breathless and a little dizzy when Harper stands and steps into my arms. "You killed me. Give me a minute."

She chuckles, her cheeks flushed pink. "It's fine. You don't have to return the favor just because I did that for you. I'm not keeping score."

I give her a pointed look. "Well, I am. And I'm sure as hell returning the favor. As soon as I can move again."

She nestles in even closer, and I tighten my arms around her, holding her tight.

At the risk of sounding dramatic, I've never had anything like this. Shit, I've never had anything even *remotely* like this with a woman. And maybe that should scare me, but so far, I'm just happy. Like stupid happy.

And once I regain the feeling in my body, I make Harper as happy as she's made me—or maybe even happier, because she screams out my name pretty damn loud when she comes on my tongue.

Later, after we've cuddled for a while in my bed, Harper announces that she's hungry. We head to the kitchen in search of some snacks, and end up breaking into a gift basket I received from the team, full of hummus and pita, cheese and crackers, chocolate chip cookies, and dried fruit. We have a little bit of everything while sitting at the kitchen island. Harper sips from a glass of wine, and I crack open a bottle of IPA.

I listen while Harper complains about the article she's just been hired to write, another tech piece on millennials. "What kinds of things do you want to write?"

She shrugs. "It doesn't matter. Right now, I just write what pays the bills."

I turn her face toward mine. "It matters to me. Tell me, baby."

With a soft inhale, Harper meets my eyes. "I want to write a novel someday. An epic love story."

I smile. "Then you should."

She gives me a shy look. "I wouldn't have the first clue about how to begin."

"I don't believe that for a second. You're the most determined person I've ever met. You could do it. I'm sure of it."

"It's a stupid dream, Jordie. Do you know how many people dream about writing a book and getting it published? A whole heck of a lot. And do you know how many can actually make a living doing it?"

I shrug.

"Very few."

"Yeah, but people said the same thing to me when I was growing up, that playing professional hockey was way out of reach. But it wasn't. Not for me. And I don't think writing is out of reach for you. I've read some of your work, Harper. It's really fucking good."

"You have?" Her voice is filled with surprise.

I nod. "I looked up your byline and read a bunch of the articles you've done. You're an amazing writer. Funny and witty and relatable."

"Well, thank you, but that doesn't mean I have what it takes to write a novel."

Shaking my head, I say, "Don't count yourself out. That's all I'm saying."

Harper pops a disgusting green olive into her mouth and chews with a satisfied hum.

"Damn, baby. You were so perfect until that moment." I frown at her.

"What?" she asks with a chuckle.

"Olives are disgusting."

She shakes her head, emphatic. "No way. I love olives."

I shudder and make a gagging sound.

"Shut up." She shoves two hands against my chest, but I'm an immovable wall of muscle, and I merely laugh at her attempts.

It feels so natural being here with Harper. Teasing her. Watching her move around my kitchen dressed in one of my old T-shirts.

"Here." I shove the jar of olives toward her. "You might as well eat up. I can't stand these things."

She smirks and pops another olive into her mouth. "So, can I ask you something?"

I brace myself. When someone words it that way instead of just asking their question, it's usually because it's a serious topic. "Sure."

She picks up another olive and meets my eyes. "Will you tell me about your dad?"

I pull in a deep breath and let it out slowly.

Normally, I hide my past like it's a dirty secret I can't admit to. But with Harper, it doesn't feel that way.

It's seemed so natural opening myself up to her, and I've felt total acceptance from her. No judgment whatsoever. Why I'm so comfortable around her when I couldn't even mention my dad's suicide to my best friends isn't something I understand. She just makes me feel safe, accepted, and I really love that feeling.

Obviously, things won't always be this easy. She's right about my hockey schedule being tough, but I want to prove to her that I can do this. That I can commit fully to her, and be the best boyfriend in the whole fucking world.

"Jordie?" she whispers, meeting my eyes.

"I guess so. I don't really talk about him, but for you, I will."

She touches my hand and gives me a sympathetic look. "What was he like? Did he like hockey?"

I grin at a sudden memory of my dad in the stands at one of my pee-wee hockey games. "Yeah, he loved it. He was really proud of me." I look at the cabinet behind her, hesitating.

"I'll bet he was," she says encouragingly.

I push the package of cookies across the counter toward Harper since she's abandoned the olives now, but she doesn't take one. She just keeps watching me.

"One thing I loved about him . . ." I suck in a deep breath before continuing. "After a game, other kids' parents would be picking apart their performance, commenting on how their son should have done this or that differently, but my dad never did that. Even the times I played like shit, and he could have pointed that out, he always just said the same thing every time we got in the car."

"What did he say?" she whispers.

"That it was a pleasure watching me play."

Harper stands suddenly to wrap me in her arms, and I rest my chin on the top of her head while she presses her cheek over my heart. "That's a beautiful memory."

A lump lodges itself in my throat, and I nod, blinking hard. "Yeah."

Fuck. It even hurts to remember the good stuff. This right here is why I don't let myself think about him. Well, I still think about him almost every day. Something random will pop into my head, but I push it away in a big damn hurry so I don't have to *feel* anything.

"I wish he didn't have to go." My voice is barely above a whisper, and I feel Harper's head bob as she nods, her cheek still pressed to the front of my T-shirt.

"I know he would have stayed if he could have. He must have been really tired of fighting."

I nod, feeling numb. *God, how is she so insightful?* As painful as this is, I'm glad Harper knows. I'm glad she's aware of this part of me. Because as much as I try to deny it, his loss will always be a big part of me.

After another few minutes of hugging it out, Harper pulls back and meets my eyes. "Guess what?" Her voice is cheerful now, and I'm thankful for the distraction and change of subject.

I smile. "What?"

"I have some exciting news."

I touch her cheek, turning her face toward mine. "Tell me."

"You know your twelve-day trip that's coming up?"

I nod. It'll be a bear of a trip. We start in Ohio, then move on to Illinois, Michigan, Pennsylvania, New Jersey, and New York. It's a six-game, twelve-day journey, the longest in our franchise's history. It's going to be brutal, both mentally and physically, but it's also going to be hell because I'll be away from her.

"Yes, but how do *you* know about my twelve-day trip? Your dad?"

"Kind of. He pulled some strings and got me an assignment covering the Ice Hawks during the trip. It's sort of an all-access look at the team, and a behind-the-scenes of everything that goes on during the trip."

It's the last thing I expected her to say, but also the best thing I've ever heard. "No fucking way. So you're coming with us?"

Smiling, she nods. "Is that okay with you?"

A huge grin overtakes my face, and I practically tackle her with a hug. "Are you kidding? That's fucking awesome."

With a laugh, Harper relaxes against me.

"Did you have enough to eat?" I ask, my gaze locked on hers.

She nods and opens her mouth to speak, but she doesn't get a word out before I lift her in my arms and begin stalking back toward my bedroom with her.

Last week, I asked our team doctor to give me a test for sexually transmitted diseases. At first, he looked confused, and then he asked what symptoms I was experiencing. I assured him there were none, that I was in a monogamous relationship and wanted to assure my girl I was clean so we could ditch the condoms if she wanted that too, since she's on birth control.

Yesterday, the test results finally landed in my email, confirming that I'm good to go.

I hope Harper's ready for that step like I am. I want her to know I'm serious about us and our future. I wouldn't do that for just any girl. It's crazy, because I've only known her for a short time, but she's the first girl I can really see myself settling down with. Maybe that should scare me—but it doesn't. Not in the slightest.

I set her on her feet at the end of my bed. The air between us crackles with sexual attraction, but it's more than that. I need her, but it's not just a physical need. I've lied to myself for so long. I have emotional needs too, and Harper is satisfying all of them in ways I never imagined I'd want.

"Get naked, baby."

Harper shimmies out of her underwear and pulls the oversized T-shirt off over her head. She's gorgeous. She's got the body of a woman, not a gym rat. She's soft and curvy, and I love it. I'm hard and straining for her already.

"Get a condom," she whispers, climbing onto my bed, flashing me the hottest view ever as she crawls up toward the pillows.

I drop my pants and join her, placing one knee on the mattress. "I got tested. The results are in my email. I was going to show you." *God, shut up, Jordie.* I'm rambling, and it's the least romantic sentence ever, but Harper only smiles.

"I trust you." Her words pierce straight through me. Then she reaches out and rubs my erection through my briefs. Kneading and squeezing.

I manage a shaky inhale as desire slices through me. When I tug my shirt off over my head, her gaze moves lower, tracing my abdomen again and the wicked-looking bruises over my ribs. She reaches out with one fingertip, lightly touching the welt.

"Be careful with me," I murmur, suddenly feeling way the fuck out of my element.

"I'll always be careful with you," she says solemnly.

My heart goes *splat*.

God, this girl.

I lie back and Harper climbs on top of me, perched above me like a goddess. I touch her breasts and run my hands along her sides. When she joins us, I let out a slow hiss at how tight and hot she feels with nothing between us.

Pleasure rockets through me. "Oh *shit*."

I groan. It's way too much, like bringing a bazooka to a fistfight. I need to stop her. But, of course I don't. I can't.

"Jordie . . ." She moans, touching her breasts. She moves slowly, grinding her delicious body on top of mine in a way that makes her shiver in my arms.

"I love that," I manage to say, my voice uncharacteristically soft. "Fuck, it feels incredible."

"Good. Because I could do this all night." Her lips tilt into a satisfied smile.

My hands settle on her hips, and I use the leverage to fuck her deeper. With a needy sound, Harper quickens her pace.

"That's it." I groan, loving watching her. "Ride me, baby."

One more little gasp and Harper falls onto my chest, her body gripping mine in wave after wave of pleasure. Her promise of doing this all night is broken, but I don't care. She feels so good.

I've never felt this much. Been this raw.

I follow her over the edge, my climax an explosion. She collapses onto me, and I hold her close, my heartbeat erratic.

"That was incredible," she says, breathing hard before she climbs off me. "Be right back."

She heads into the adjoining master bath. After a moment, I hear the toilet flush, and the water running. And then Harper is standing gloriously naked in the doorway, giving me a shy smile.

The way she looks at me, *damn*. I know I sound sappy as shit, but it makes my breath catch. I never expected to feel this much for her, but I do. I really fucking do. And now that I know what this feeling is—not that I'm ready to say the words out loud—there's no way I'm going to let her go.

I let out a shaky laugh. "Get over here."

She moves toward me, and my heart squeezes in my chest. And when she climbs into bed beside me, everything is right in the world.

CHAPTER EIGHTEEN

Game Over

Jordie

When your team captain hits a major career milestone, the team leadership makes a really big deal about it. Tonight there's a dinner party to honor Grant, who will play his one thousandth game tomorrow night to a sold-out arena. Thankfully, Harper agreed to be my date, so I'm not alone here like I normally am at team events.

All the guys chipped in, and we bought Grant a surprise golfing trip to Scotland, our way of saying *congrats and thanks for being a great captain*. He's thirty-four now, and I can't help but wonder how many more years of hockey he has in him. Especially now that he has a kid and another on the way—I know he hates leaving Hunter and Ana. I would too if I had someone to come home to every night.

But I'd like to think Harper and I are moving in the right direction. I know she resisted jumping into a relationship with me, and I know she has her reasons why—and they're totally valid. But our chemistry is impossible to ignore. So I'd like to think it's less that I've worn her down, and more that she's realized how well we work together.

The restaurant is a fancy steakhouse downtown with a large private room in the back reserved just for us. Dozens of players and their plus-ones are mingling, standing around in small groups, chatting before dinner is served. Later, we'll have speeches and a slideshow of Grant's career highlights, but right now there are gin and tonics to drink—and I even remembered to order Harper's with a slice of cucumber, just like she did the first night we met.

As gorgeous as Harper looked that first night we met in that frosty blue dress, tonight she's on a whole other level. Dressed in a formfitting red cocktail dress that shows off all her curves, she's stunning. It's a miracle I can string together coherent sentences with all the blood rushing from my head to my groin.

"You trying to torture me in that dress?" I groan, leaning in and resting one hand against the small of her back.

Her lips lift in a mischievous smile. "What's wrong with my dress?"

I give her a stern look, playfully raising one eyebrow. "Other than the fact that it's making my pants too tight . . . not a damn thing." Memories of that night in my truck, and then later in her bed, replay on a constant loop in my brain, making concentrating on anything else but Harper nearly impossible.

"Jordie," she says, chiding me as she swats my shoulder with one manicured hand. "My dad is right over there."

It's true. He is. I glance over to where Coach Allen is standing with Coach Dodd and Coach Bryant. Harper's dad looks up just then as if someone called his name, and he smiles when he sees Harper and me together.

I give him a little wave, and Harper does the same.

"I should probably go thank your dad at some point for giving me your number and making all my dreams come true."

She chuckles and rolls her eyes. "Quit being

cheesy."

Maybe it's the fact that my team is doing well this season, or maybe it's that we're here to celebrate one of the best men I know, but damn, I'm happier than I've been in a long time. Maybe in my whole adult life.

Hell, even as I have those thoughts, I know they're excuses. I'm happy because of the gorgeous woman standing beside me.

"I know, that was a bad line. But I'm happy. Like really happy."

She softens, her gaze meeting mine, and I feel the familiar crackle of electricity buzzing between us. "I am too."

She's agreed to sleep over at my place tonight, and to say I'm looking forward to later would be a massive understatement.

Over the past month, I've learned so much about Harper. She likes her coffee with lots of cream and just a dash of sugar. She likes olives, green the most, but black too. She believes in love, even if she resisted the idea that she could find it with me. She's a daddy's girl, although she probably wouldn't admit it. Babies scare her, but she still regularly volunteers to babysit for her sister.

Every new detail I discover about Harper only makes me want to know more.

I know she wants to be a writer more than anything, and that part of her is afraid to fail. I know she'll succeed, though. She's smart and fierce, and she'll accomplish whatever she sets her mind to. Of that, I have little doubt.

I touch her cheek and turn her face toward mine to steal a chaste kiss.

"I'm going to go say hi to Elise," Harper says.

I nod, not at all surprised she knows Elise. She's our goalie's younger sister, and is engaged to Justin Brady, our starting center.

"Tell her I said hello."

Harper nods. "Will do."

I wander over to join a few of the guys who are predictably hanging out near the appetizers.

"Hey, Jordie," Teddy says, smiling when he sees me. "When's the next book club meeting?"

I chuckle. "You actually want to meet again? You realize I won't be paying you."

He grins. "Hell yeah, I want to meet again. I tried a few of those moves from the book with

Sara, and it was fucking *hot*."

"You know I only did that to impress Harper, right?"

He shrugs. "I know. But I figured it was worth asking."

I chuckle and watch Harper chat with the hockey wives across the room. My gaze makes a lazy sweep of her curves, landing on her flawless face. *Fuck*. I'm a lucky bastard.

Morgan wanders over to where we're standing and raises his pint glass in my direction. An unexpected knot tightens in my stomach.

"Well, Jordie, you actually did it," he says with a grin. "You got her to fall for you."

The strange urge to hit something flares up inside me. I never should have made that stupid bet. I didn't even know Harper then, and the juvenile need to impress the guys took precedence. *Fuck*, I was stupid.

"Keep your money. The bet was a stupid idea." My throat tightens as I choke out the words. "I don't want it."

Morgan laughs and shakes his head. "No way. I've got ten Benjamins right here for you." He fishes a wad of cash out of his pocket and tries to hand it to me—a thousand dollars that I don't want or need.

I curl my fist tighter around my drink, glaring at him. "I don't want your money."

"Drop it, dude," Teddy says, giving him a stern look, but Morgan just laughs.

"A bet's a bet. Jordie got Coach's icy daughter to fall for him. He won fair and square."

We realize a second too late that Harper has made her way over to join us. When I meet her eyes, all I can see is her pain and humiliation reflected back at me. It's like taking a puck to the chest—all the air leaves my lungs at once, and I feel breathless.

"Harper," I say, but she raises one trembling hand before I can continue.

"A bet?" Her voice is unsteady and filled with hurt.

A jolt of pain zings through me, and I stagger half a step back like I've been slapped.

"That's all this was to you? Getting me to date you was because of a bet with the guys?"

I open my mouth to respond, but Harper's already fleeing. With tears brimming in her eyes, she's turned and stumbles away.

I want to yell. I want to scream and kick and punch. Instead, I stand here feeling miserable while my friends watch with looks of pity.

Every muscle in my body clenches, and a heavy weight settles in the pit of my stomach.

Anger and disappointment rage inside me. It's not just anger—no, it's rejection. Burning and stinging and so all-consuming, it almost knocks me over. I've waited my whole life to meet a girl like Harper, a woman who would make me want to settle down and commit, to be a better man. And now I have.

Harper.

With a shuddering inhale, I press the heels of my palms against my eyes, staving off the tears that threaten.

God, what have I done?

CHAPTER NINETEEN

Nothing Breaks Like a Heart

Harper

My heart is pounding so hard, I can feel my pulse in every inch of my body, and my stomach is tied up in knots.

I can't believe this is happening.

My throat's caving in and I can barely breathe. The only complete thought I can form is, *How the hell do I get out of here?* It's like time has slowed to an absolute standstill, and everything else falls away, except for the one small piece of reality I just can't quite process right now.

Jordie is a liar.

This whole thing—us—was a lie. A complete sham. A freaking *bet* with his asshole teammates.

How could I have been so stupid?

Searching frantically for an escape route, I can't stop the panic that threatens to take hold of me. Were there always so many people here? Why does this room suddenly feel so goddamn small? I squeeze past a couple of guys who are too busy laughing to notice the tearstained mess having a panic attack beside them.

Figures. They're hockey players. What did I expect?

Why was I so stupid?

My gaze finally lands on the door, and I barrel toward it, ignoring the smiling faces around me and Jordie's booming voice calling my name behind me.

Once I make it out of the room, I weave through the crowded restaurant to the exit. Did they have to pick a noisy steakhouse on a Saturday night? I force a weak smile at the bubbly hostess, who looks surprised and slightly horrified at the sight of me. When I finally push the heavy glass door open, the cold night air is a welcome relief.

"Have a good night!" the hostess calls after me as the door closes.

I wipe the tears from my cheeks and take a deep, steadying breath. I haven't felt this bad, this panicked, since I was told my dad was in the hospital. And even that was different. Because this? This is like a sucker punch to the gut *and* a piano falling out of the sky, and I'm the clueless little cartoon character who should have seen it coming.

I'm fishing in my purse for my car keys when the door behind me bursts open, and Jordie's deep, strained voice cuts through the quiet.

"Harper, wait," he says, begging me. "Please, let me explain."

Turning quickly, I face him, and it's like the piano's dropping on me all over again.

How is it that he's allowed to look so devastated right now? I'm the one who's been hurt. I'm the one who looks like an idiot. I'm the one his teammates are probably laughing about right now. Jordie doesn't get to be upset right now. It's not fair.

But he is upset. His eyes are filled with emotion, and his mouth is drawn into a line. Even his hair is a mess, like he raked his fingers through it in frustration.

It doesn't take long for my hurt to boil over into anger.

"Well? Is it true?" I ask sharply, staring at him expectantly.

"Harper, please, it's not what you think." He reaches for my hand, but I recoil, taking a step back and crossing my arms.

"What is it then? Because I think you made a bet with your buddies. That's all this was to you, all I was to you—a game."

"It wasn't a game to me, and you sure as fuck were never a game. Yes, it might have started out that way, but then—"

I cut him off with a startled cry as fresh, hot tears spill down my cheeks. "And then, what, you upped the ante? Two hundred bucks if you got me to go out with you, five hundred if you got in my pants?"

God, this is all so high school. So immature and ridiculous. But it hurts all the same, because I thought what we had was real. *Stupid me.*

"No, it was never like that. I'm so sorry. Please, just—"

"I can't do this right now."

There's no way I'm wasting any more time or tears on this asshole. As soon as my fingers land on my keys, I storm to the car, leaving Jordie standing on the curb, his face in his hands, one of his teammates appearing by his side.

I drive home in silence. No radio and no more tears. I've already begun my mantra for self-healing.

It was never going to work out anyway. You're too good for him.

I try to tell myself it's better this way, and that I was right about him all along. I can learn from this situation and do better in the future with who I decide to let in.

But nothing I tell myself will untie the knot that keeps growing in my stomach, or stop my heart from rising higher into my throat. It's practically choking me, and I'm gasping for air.

When I get to my apartment, I can't help but feel silly when I see my reflection in the window. These heels, this red dress. I was playing right into Jordie's game.

I've just made it inside and locked the door behind me when I hear loud, determined footsteps approaching, and I don't need to look through the peephole to know who it is.

"Harper! I'm so sorry! Please, just let me talk to you!" Jordie's voice carries down the hallway, and I can feel my heart rate pick back up again.

"Go away, Jordie!" I call back without thinking about my neighbors. I'm not rational, levelheaded Harper anymore. I'm hurt, angry, humiliated Harper now, and she has no problem if the neighbors hear her yelling at a man outside.

Jordie knocks on my door and calls out my name, but I do my best to tune him out. Sure, I've been hurt before, but something about this betrayal is different. It stings. It burns. It makes me worry I'll never trust another man again.

"Harper, I'm so sorry. Will you please give me a chance to explain?"

Despite how incredibly angry I am with him, I can't ignore the hurt in his voice. I've never heard him this way before. Pleading. Upset. Desperate.

I walk back to the door, wrapping my arms around myself, and take a deep breath. "I don't know what's left to explain," I say, just loud enough for him to hear me on the other side of the two inches of wood between us.

"Okay, fine. Yes, this relationship started out as a bet," he says.

I wince, closing my eyes. "Got that much, thanks."

"But from the moment I first got to know you, it stopped being about that."

"What was it about then?"

"You. Us," he says in almost a whisper.

I swallow another wave of hot emotion as my stomach squeezes.

"Being with you has changed me, Harper."

I scoff, shaking my head. "Yeah, it changed you into a liar who doesn't seem to have a problem with using people to impress his bros."

"I fucked up. You're right. I never should have accepted the bet to begin with. I didn't know anything about you when I made it—I didn't even know you were the coach's daughter. It was stupid and reckless, but I did it anyway, and there's nothing I can do to change that."

I don't respond. How the hell does he think I'm supposed to react to that?

"Are you still there?" he asks softly, his voice filled with worry.

"This is pointless, Jordie." I sigh. "It's *over*,

okay? You had your fun, and you've got your money. Now you just need to leave me alone."

"I don't think I can do that."

"That's not your decision anymore. Go home, Jordie."

The words taste bitter coming out of my mouth, but Jordie must sense their finality. Because when I put my hand on the doorknob and carefully pull it open, ready to find him standing there, for him to sweep me up in his arms and make everything okay . . .

He's gone.

CHAPTER TWENTY

Down and Out

Jordie

The next few days pass by in a painful blur. I've barely moved, rotating only between my couch and my bed. I haven't shaved or showered, and the smell coming from my T-shirt is proof of that. I've only gotten up to use the bathroom, or to answer the door for the take-out food I've been living on for the past three days. I look like shit, but I feel even worse.

Shifting on the couch, I grab my phone. I have a couple of missed calls from Grant and Owen, and an unread text message from my sister. But no response to the dozens of text messages and phone calls I've made to Harper. The evening after Grant's party, I went to the coffee shop where she has her book club meetings, but she wasn't there.

On Wednesday, I went to the animal shelter, only to find out she wasn't volunteering. They said it was the first time she'd ever called in sick in two years.

After I realized that she was breaking up with me, that I'd missed my shot with her, I headed home—and holed up here like the loser I am.

Empty take-out containers and bottles of beer litter the coffee table in front of me, and I roll over on the couch, tugging one of the pillows over my head. I have practice tomorrow, which means I'm going to be forced to leave my apartment.

I consider showering. Consider cleaning up the disgusting mess of my apartment, but I don't do either. I just shuffle back to my bedroom and collapse onto the mattress.

I've never been in a real relationship, never let myself grow close enough with a woman to get my heart broken like this, but *damn*. Now that I have? Now that I've experienced something deep and meaningful with Harper? *Shit*, this is painful.

My heart throbs once in my chest, as if to remind me it's still there, and I rub at the tender spot. Even though I'm exhausted, mentally and physically, I know sleep won't come easily tonight. How do I know that? Because I've barely slept a few hours over the past few nights combined.

I need to fix this. But how? Because, *fuck*. I really messed up. I feel empty and lost and so broken. And it's made all the worse by the fact that this is completely my fault.

It's with that lonely, awful thought that I close my eyes and try to sleep.

• • •

In the morning, I force myself to get dressed and ready for practice. On the drive there, I've never felt more miserable and less excited about heading to the ice. I can't even climb into my truck without being assaulted by memories of what Harper and I did right here in the driver's seat.

I finally had a shot at something real with the most incredible woman, and I fucked it all up by being immature and competitive. But Harper was never a game to me—she was everything.

At the training facility, I'm just finishing taping up my shin pads when Grant stops beside me in the locker room.

"You look like shit."

I swallow. "Thanks."

He huffs out a sigh and sits down beside me. "You doing okay, rookie?"

I ignore his question and tear off another piece of athletic tape. "How's Ana feeling?"

"About the same."

"That sucks."

He makes a pensive sound. "I feel so guilty when we travel. I hate leaving, knowing she still has to care for Hunter while she's sick and miserable. I feel like a dick for leaving her alone."

I nod absently. I've been so caught up in my own problems, I forgot other people are dealing with things too. "That's rough. What about hiring a nanny or something? To help out when you're gone?"

Grant shakes his head. "Ana doesn't want to. She thinks she can do it all."

"That sounds like Ana." I still couldn't believe that night they invited me over, she cooked a full meal after being violently ill. I still feel terrible about that. But, *damn*, those bison tacos were good.

He nods. "Once she's out of the first trimester, which will be soon, she should start feeling better. This pregnancy has been really different from her first one, so we're just guessing as we go."

"Well, if there's anything I can do to help . . ."

I don't get to finish that sentence because Grant levels me with a serious look. "You and I both know you have your own shit to deal with. I heard some of the guys talking."

"You heard about the bet then? And that Harper hates me?" There's no use trying to dance around the issue. Besides, Grant would get the truth out of me eventually. He always does.

He grabs his mouth guard and stands, meeting my eyes with a stern expression. "Yeah, I heard. Are you doing all right?"

"Honestly? No."

He puts one hand on my shoulder and gives me a fatherly look of disappointment. His opinion means more to me than anyone's, and I suddenly feel even worse. Disappointing Grant is the last thing I wanted to do. The dark look in his eyes is too much, and I glance away as unease swims inside me. But when Grant speaks again, his voice is calm, clear.

"You made a mistake. But maybe there's still a way you can make it right."

With a sigh, I rise to my feet. "Yeah, I doubt that."

When we take to the ice, I try to clear my head and focus, but it's hard. And the way Harper's dad looks at me with disgust makes me feel even worse. He shows no mercy, making me sprint across the ice every chance he gets until I'm puking in a trash can beside the ice. And the thing is, I totally deserve it.

• • •

The next day, I'm on a plane to Boston to play a series of games in the Atlantic Division. I'm hoping it's just the distraction I need. Growing up, when things got tough, hockey was always there for me. I need tonight to be that way again, because I don't know how much longer I can handle feeling this way.

I manage to score a goal on the ice tonight, and after the game, the first person I want to tell is Harper. My phone chimes with a text, and I scramble for it, hoping it's her. But it's Tiffany instead.

Congratulations, little broth-
        er! I'm proud of you.

My heart sinks. She wouldn't be proud of me if she knew what I did. That I drove Harper away by placing that stupid bet, by making her think this was all some game to me, when in truth, it wasn't. Not at all.

I got the date I wanted—*shit*, the date I practically *begged* her for. And I had sex with her, and it was so much better than I ever even imagined. But the crazy thing is, all I want in the world is the chance to see Harper smile at me again, to hear her laugh at something I say or roll her eyes when I make a stupid comment.

For as many confusing thoughts that are ricocheting around in my head, one thought is the loudest.

I wish my dad were here.

I could really use his advice right now. Even though he'd probably scowl at me, he'd also help me figure out what the fuck I can do to make this right.

Feeling lost, I swallow. With a deep exhale, I realize there is someone else I could talk to. Harper's dad. Plus, I obviously owe him a huge apology for hurting his daughter.

Before I can chicken out, I grab my phone and

dial his number.

"Coach Allen?" I say when he answers. "It's Jordan Prescott."

"Yeah. What did you need?"

I hesitate, scrubbing one hand over the stubble on my jaw. "Can we talk?"

There's a long pause, and then he releases a slow breath. "Of course we can, kid."

CHAPTER TWENTY-ONE

Playing the Game

Harper

My dad knows I don't want to go on this trip, but he also knows that once I commit to something, I see it through. Plus, I'm not particularly in the place financially to be turning down paid writing assignments.

Dad really went out on a limb to get me a coveted assignment on the team's longest road trip this season. Six cities. Twelve days. Nearly two weeks of having to endure seeing the man who broke my heart.

I finish packing my bag and order an Uber. The plane takes off in an hour from a private airstrip at the airport.

Since I'm not sure what to expect, I've packed

a variety of options—jeans and sweatshirts, a black suit in case I feel like looking businesslike, and a cocktail dress and tights in case we go to dinner somewhere fancy. Then I grab my gray wool coat and give my apartment one last look.

"See you in twelve days," I mutter.

I hope.

Unless having to be constantly surrounded by Jordie and his teammates kills me.

When I reach the airport, the driver is as unfamiliar with where I'm supposed to be as I am, and so it takes us a few minutes of circling the airstrip to find the right hangar. The car parks in the small lot and I climb out, grabbing my rolling suitcase from the trunk before he can get out to assist me.

"I got it, thanks," I call to the driver.

Dad is standing on the airstrip, smiling as he watches me approach. I stop before him, and he pulls me into a hug.

"I'm proud of you, Harper," he says, emotion in his voice.

He knows things didn't work out between Jordie and me, but he doesn't know the details. At least, he didn't learn them from me, and he hasn't asked any questions. I'm grateful for that, because I certainly don't feel like offering up any details.

I nod once. "Anywhere special I should sit?" I look up at the impressive jet in the distance.

"Up front. Next to me."

I follow Dad toward the plane while my stomach ties itself in a gigantic knot. Keeping my gaze down, I board the plane and settle into my seat.

"You okay?" Dad asks from beside me, looking concerned.

Deep breaths, Harper.

"Whatever doesn't kill you . . ." I force my lips into a grim smile, and Dad pats my knee.

I don't think I'm fooling anyone, but I'll die trying.

God, what is with all these death analogies?

Needing to clear my head, I pull a pen and notebook from my purse. Just having them in my hands centers me the tiniest bit. Dad gives me another one of his encouraging smiles and a pat on the leg before tapping away at his iPad.

Focusing on the reason I'm here, I put pen to paper. As the plane climbs to its cruising altitude, I scribble down a few notes.

If you look up the characteristics of someone with high testosterone, you will find things like tough-minded, direct, decisive, competitive, and also . . . emotionally contained. It's practically a road map for understanding hockey players. Tough? Check. Valiant competitors? Check. Unable to express an emotion if their life depended on it? Uh-huh, that too.

I look up and turn in my seat, and my gaze finds Jordie toward the back of the plane. He's sitting beside Grant, and Owen and Justin are turned toward them. They're all discussing something in low tones. Owen laughs at something that's said. But my focus is on Jordie, and even though it's painful to look at him, I allow myself to drink him in for just a moment longer.

His normally stoic face is softened as he sits huddled with his teammates. Not discussing hockey, but just being guys. I see then what hasn't occurred to me before. This is his family. These are the people who matter to him.

I'm glad he has them. I know his family relationships aren't as close as he would have liked. But at least he has this.

• • •

Three days later, I'm invited to attend a team dinner. A big part of me wants to refuse when Dad extends the invitation, because all I want to do is hole up in my hotel room.

My pride won't let me do that, though. I can't let Jordie think he's broken me, and that I'm crying into my pillow every night.

And that's why I now find myself at a Middle Eastern restaurant in Detroit, surrounded by the entire team and coaching staff. The food is fragrant and incredible, but I barely manage a few bites of hummus and chicken shawarma.

Dad nudges me under the table. "Maybe you should talk to him?"

I don't bother to ask who he's referring to. I also don't dare look in the direction of where Jordie's seated—at the far end of the table. Whenever we've been in the same location, he's always stayed as far away from me as possible. Whether that's due to my perpetual resting bitch face or his own guilt, I'm not sure.

"There's nothing to say," I mutter under my breath.

"No? You sure about that?" Dad gives me a look—a stern, fatherly look—and I focus my attention on my plate.

Jordie's played like shit in the games against Columbus and Chicago. I'm sure Dad only wants to make sure his star rookie can get his head back in the game. But I'm not going to forgive Jordie just so he can start playing better hockey. *Fuck that.*

When dinner is over, I'm standing beside Dad while he signs for the check. Most of the players have already filtered out of the restaurant.

Jordie approaches and stops beside me, and the familiar scent of his cologne makes my heart throb and flashes of our time together slam through me.

"I'll be outside," Dad says, stepping away to give us a moment.

With a steadying breath, I turn to face Jordie. He's beautiful. Staggeringly so. And he looks visibly haunted. Dark circles under his eyes. Mouth turned down in a frown. He shoves his hands in his pockets, like he's doing it to avoid reaching out and touching me.

Good thing, too, because I could never handle the feel of his calloused fingers on my skin. I'm barely holding it together as it is.

"I've wanted to talk to you. How are you?" he says, his deep voice washing over me.

"I've been okay," I say softly, and it's sort of the truth. I've gotten out of bed every day. I've forced a few bites of food into my mouth at every meal. I've smiled when I was supposed to so Dad won't worry. But I have no idea when this is supposed to stop hurting so much.

Jordie clears his throat. "That's . . . good to hear."

"Did you need something? I should really get back to the hotel." I tip my head toward where my dad is standing near the hostess station.

"I have something I need to say. Something I want to tell you."

"Okay." My voice is shaky. *Breathe, Harper.*

"You know what my sister said when I told her about you, told her there was a woman I was excited about?"

I shift, steeling myself. I'm still far too raw to be standing here in the middle of a busy restaurant, having a conversation with this man. My nerves are so frazzled, I've barely been able to eat or sleep, and now he wants to casually rehash our entire relationship. Right now?

Fuck, this is painful.

"What?" I manage to say past the lump in my throat.

"She was scared I was going to mess it up and get hurt. It's what I do."

It's not what I expected him to say. "Why would she say that?"

He looks down like he doesn't want to say the words on the tip of his tongue.

"Jordie?" I say softly, prompting him.

He meets my gaze again, and the breath is sucked from my lungs. His eyes are a brutal shade of blue, and they see everything. *Everything*. Right down to the very core of me. It's unnerving, and I feel a little unsteady on my feet.

"She was sure it'd all fall apart, because I'd chosen a woman who was emotionally unavailable. Just like our mother."

My ragged heart breaks just a little bit more. That's not true, is it? "Jordie . . ."

He licks his lips, his fists shoving deeper inside his pockets. "She was wrong about that, for the record. But she was right about me. This never could have worked. I was always going to fuck it up, and now I have. And for that, I'm truly sorry. All I ever wanted was for you to be happy, and to be the man who enhanced your happiness."

I nod once, unshed tears stinging my eyes.

For a month, Jordie and I enjoyed a steady diet of sex and late-night talks, and we grew close as a result. Closer than I ever thought possible.

And now my heart is shattered.

"Take care of yourself, Harper," he says in that deep, throaty voice I've grown to love.

I nod once, and then I turn and flee like a coward, because he doesn't deserve to see me cry.

CHAPTER TWENTY-TWO
One Big Tangled Mess

Jordie

I haven't spoken to Harper in a few days, not since I approached her at the restaurant in Detroit.

Once upon a time, we were both so excited she was coming along on this road trip. I envisioned her in the stands, cheering me on, and sneaking into her hotel room to make love any chance I got. Of course, the reality has been so much different. We've had exactly one five-minute conversation, and even that was hard as fuck. The memory of that sad smile she tossed my way makes my heart twist.

Fuck. Get a grip.

Maybe this whole thing between us was doomed from the start, meant to fall apart since it all began based on a lie. A ridiculous bet I've regretted ever since the day I made it.

As I've gotten older, I've started to realize a few things. My physical strength will fade, and hockey will eventually come to an end. Youth, beauty . . . all of it will fade with time.

But love? Love will remain. And that's what I want.

I want something that won't wither away. I want something steady, something that will last. I want someone to choose me, and not just because of what I can do with a stick and a puck. I want unconditional love. And so far, it's eluded me.

"How are you doing?" Grant asks, fixing his intense gray eyes on mine.

I look away. We got back to our hotel room an hour ago. It's the final night of our trip, and I think we're both ready for it to be over. Him for very different reasons than mine. He has someone he's desperate to get back to. Me, not so much. The only thing waiting for me in Seattle is an empty apartment.

"Fine. And you?"

He scoffs. "The truth, Jordie. How are you?"

"I'm fucking fantastic, dude. Seriously," I say, forcing out the words on a frustrated exhale.

Needing to move, I head to the sliding glass doors in our hotel room and pull them open, letting the cool air rush over me. Grant follows me out onto the balcony, unwilling to take a hint. It's cold, and my hoodie does little to shelter me from the breeze. He leans one hip against the railing, looking at me while I drop into one of the chairs.

I push my hands into my hair and look out at the New York City skyline. "What the fuck am I going to do, man?"

He gives me a sad smile. "Easy. Fix it."

I huff out a humorless laugh. "Oh yeah, real fucking simple. She won't even speak to me."

"Then find a way to make her listen."

Sure, real simple. The last time I tried, she barely tolerated a few minutes of idle conversation

I guess it was just a stupid fantasy thinking that Harper could be mine, that she might be my forever. God, I can't even believe I entertained that idea. But I did, I *really* did, and it would have been so easy to picture . . .

Harper smiling by my side. Her in the wives and girlfriends' box at my games. Us lounging at home, cooking together, grocery shopping. And then later, me with an engagement ring box in my pocket, getting down on one knee, promising to love her until the end of forever. Harper tearing up, her lips pressing to mine . . .

A lump rises in my throat at the thought. God, I'm being ridiculous. Maybe it was never meant to be. Maybe it's better this way.

Then why do I feel like I'm about to fall apart from the pain of losing her?

Inhaling deeply, I try to force her from my mind. It's easier said than done.

Grant shifts, staring down at his phone. "Shit, the article's up."

"Huh?" I glance over at him.

"The piece Harper wrote about the team is online," he says, pointing at his phone.

Rather than snatch it from him like I want to, I pull my phone from my pocket and type Harper's name into the search bar. The article about the Ice Hawks is the first thing that comes up. The headline is ALL ACCESS TO SEATTLE'S FAVORITE BAD BOYS. There's also a photo—a couple of the guys boarding the plane, dressed in suits and overcoats. I think we were still in Ohio at that point. It was cold.

I'm not in the photo, and my gaze drops to the article below.

It's after midnight on a Thursday, and the Seattle Ice Hawks have just pulled out a win against the Columbus Admirals and are already en route to their new home for the next twenty-two hours.

Chicago.

The plane is filled with familiar favorites and new faces. Team captain, Grant Henry, is contemplative tonight, no doubt internally critiquing his team's performance as he sips a pink electrolyte drink. Meanwhile, assistant captain Teddy King entertains those around him with a colorful story set against a deep chorus of husky male laughter . . .

I remember that night. I remember boarding the plane, searching for an open seat as far away from Harper as possible. Even the scent of her shampoo set me off, squeezing something painful inside my chest.

I scan the words on the page, searching for my name. I'm not sure I'm going to find it, and then there it is.

Newcomer Jordan Prescott, known to those closest to him as Jordie, sits quietly by himself in one of the back rows, pretending to be asleep.

I smirk. How the hell did she know I was pretending? I read on, practically holding my breath for what I might find.

There's a riveting recap of the hard-fought game we played in Detroit and lost.

In Detroit, star center Justin Brady is on fire. He lays everything on the line, game after game. It's inspiring. And, quite frankly, exhausting to watch. He finds the back of the net twice, but it's still not enough to secure a victory. They have their work cut out for them. But if there's one thing these guys understand it's hard work.

Then she writes a few paragraphs about him scoring his one hundredth career goal in the day's following game.

I spot Grant's name again and make myself slow down and actually read the words, rather than skim over them in a mad rush to search out any mentions of me like I want to do.

He plays a physical brand of hockey, turning up the intensity on the ice. Contrast that with the new father Grant is off the ice, and, well, you've got yourself an emotional story arc to go along with the sports-themed one that's practically writing itself this season.

The intensity and focus that this game requires is unparalleled, and this trip in particular will test all of their endurance. Interruptions to routines, hard mattresses, and even dehydration are all concerns.

"Damn. This is good," Grant says, still reading on his phone beside me.

I nod, my mouth dry.

After taking care of business in New Jersey, the team heads to their final destination on this impressive road trip—New York.

The defending champs aren't going to hand it to them, but this team came to work, and they're not afraid to get dirty. The stakes are high and the Ice Hawks deliver, playing a physical game and dominating the first several teams they've faced off against. The heroics of starting goaltender Owen Parrish cannot be understated. He shut out the scoring opportunities in the first two games, fending off over forty shots. But it all comes down to the final away game of this grueling road trip.

I skim some more, searching for my name.

In New Jersey, it was rookie center Jordie who slapped in the winning shot with a powerful one-timer felt all the way to the rafters.

I remember that goal. Remember how I felt, that the first person I wanted to call afterward was Harper. Of course I hadn't.

There are a few more mentions of me, and every time I see my name, I jolt.

I can't believe she wrote about me. And it wasn't to curse me out or let the whole world know what a piece of shit I was. To my surprise, she didn't say a bad word about me, and believe me, she could have. She could have dragged my name through the mud if she wanted to.

But no, she wrote an insightful, intelligent piece, shedding light on the personality quirks of this team that the public doesn't get to see. I always knew Harper was a smart cookie, but this is beyond what even I expected from her. It's good. Really fucking good. Well thought out and engrossing. It's so much more than just another sports coverage article.

As soon as I finish, I read it again, and by the time I'm done, I realize Grant has gone inside. Alone, I sit there in the dark, processing everything.

After a while, the cold gets to me, and I head back inside the hotel room.

During my shower, Grant's words ring through my head. Maybe there is a way to make this right. I've got to at least try. But with Harper not wanting to talk to me, I need to figure out a way to get her attention.

Her rejection hurts more than anything. It's worse than losing a game and losing in the play-offs. But I had a coach who once told me that you learn more about yourself and what you're made of when you lose. Those words have always stuck with me because he was right.

You learn as much about who you are and what you're made of from failing as you do from success.

I may not win this one, but I will make damn sure Harper understands that I'm not a bad guy. That the bet was a huge mistake, and one I'll never repeat.

I'm down, I've had a setback, but there's no way in hell I'm going to give up and walk away. I just need to find a way to get through to her. There's a lot more game left to play, and I'm determined to win her back.

My copy of the romance novel we both read sits at the bottom of my suitcase, taunting me. I don't feel like reading about love right now, but as I stare down at the book, I get an idea. If Harper won't talk to me . . . maybe there's another way to communicate my feelings.

I grab my phone and request an Uber.

Fifteen minutes later, I'm back in my hotel room, holding the small notebook and pen I just purchased at the store. Sinking down onto the bed, I get to work writing a book for Harper.

Not a romance novel—no, I've lost that chance. What we had is no longer a romance because I set fire to it, blasted it to hell like a dumbass.

But I can write out my feelings about her, my inner thoughts, and pray that it's enough for her to forgive me.

CHAPTER TWENTY-THREE

Book Club Confessions

Harper

"I missed you!" Aurora says, raising her wine-glass in my direction.

"I missed you guys too," I say with a smile.

I got back yesterday after the grueling road trip. I'm exhausted, and all I did was tag along with the team from city to city. The guys played six grueling games of hockey on top of all that.

MK leans closer. "Was seeing your ex-lover as hard as you imagined it'd be?"

I nearly spit out my wine. "My ex-lover?"

Aurora chuckles into her fist. "We were never sure what you guys were. Did you put a label on it?"

I shrug. "Do people even do that anymore? Put labels on things? We were serious, if that's what you're asking. It was more than just physical."

MK gives me a sad look over the rim of her martini glass.

"And yeah, it was hard," I say with a frown.

Aurora gives my shoulder a squeeze.

"Your article was amazing," MK says, like that's some kind of consolation prize.

I nod. The truth is, I'm proud of my work, and it's gotten a lot of positive attention. But every time I think about that trip and writing that piece, I don't know how I'll ever feel anything but heartbroken. I couldn't even bear to read it when I was done. I just sent it off to my editor and hoped for the best.

After catching up for a while longer, on Aurora's love life and MK's data set that's been troubling her, we part ways and I head for home.

Back at my apartment, I'm feeling unsettled and finding it hard to sit still. In a moment of weakness, I type Jordie's name into a saucy puck-bunny site known for its salacious gossip. And then my breath catches because there are *a lot* of entries about Jordie. Apparently, he's a hot topic. I scroll through the posts that mention his name, and find myself growing more anxious with every second that passes.

The one titled ANYONE HAVE ANY GOSSIP ON JORDIE? catches my attention. So does the answering post once I click on it.

I wish! Apparently, the guy is a saint.

A few others comment, asking for details about where he hangs out and which bars he frequents, but there's little else. Satisfied, at least for the time being, that I'm not going to find any dirt on him, I close my laptop. But those contented feelings disappear fast as I recall a conversation Jordie and I once had.

He told me that most girls he'd gone out with in the past had already searched his name online, and that seemed to bother him—like no one wanted to get to know the guy behind the hockey helmet. Well, I did. I found out all about that guy, and it had all been one big elaborate lie. Some childish bet he'd made with his teammate.

God.

There's a knock on my door, and I slam my laptop closed like I've been caught watching porn. *Jeez, Harper.*

But I'm not expecting anyone, so I approach the door slowly and then peek through the peep-hole. There's no one there. When I open the door, I find a large manila envelope on the floor with my name on it.

With butterflies in my stomach, I carry it inside and sit down on my couch before tearing the envelope open. Inside is a black spiral notebook. I flip it open to the first page and see a note from Jordie.

Harper,

I know how much you like to read, and while I'd never be able to write a book, would you believe it if I told you I used to keep a journal? I did. All through high school. It started as my therapist's idea, and it helped me through some of my darkest days.

Since you're not currently speaking to me, and it's killing me inside, I wanted to be able to tell you every confusing thing I'm feeling. So, here goes . . .

I take a deep breath and dive in.

First, I owe you a huge apology. I never meant to hurt you. The truth is, you're the best thing that's ever happened to me. Our time together meant everything to me. I know you might not realize this, but I don't just let people in. The stuff I told you was personal. I opened up and told you things that I don't tell anyone, but I did it because I feel things for you that I haven't felt for anyone else before.

Seeing Jordie's handwriting on the pages is a bit surreal. It's neater than I imagined, slanting slightly to the left. With a smile, I recall overhearing sports announcers commenting on Jordie being lefthanded.

There are several pages about how it was torture to be so close to me on the road trip, and yet feel so far away emotionally. Tears well in my eyes because I felt the exact same way.

I devour his words, reading through the tears that blur my vision. When I turn the page, I'm shocked to find his teammates wrote notes too.

What the . . .

One from Grant reads:

Jordie's a fucking idiot. But he loves you. Even if he hasn't said it yet—he loves you. Maybe give him another chance?

And another, this one from Morgan, in which he apologizes profusely for his part in that stupid bet. He says it wasn't Jordie's idea, and that it was made before Jordie even spoke his first words to me or knew who I was.

Surprisingly, that does make me feel a tiny bit better.

There's a note from Owen. And Justin. And one from Teddy that makes me laugh.

You're probably too good for him, but maybe give the guy a second chance?

The final page contains something I don't expect. One last note from Jordie.

I'll be at the coffee shop on Wednesday night. Seven o'clock. I hope you'll join me. I hope we can talk about everything. I have no expectations beyond that. I know it's entirely possible you're done with this relationship, but please talk to me, Harper. Please do me that one favor.

Yours,

Jordie

As I stare down at his words, I realize with a sad smile that he's requesting a book club meeting with me. A meeting to discuss this book he's written me.

I have no idea if my sad little heart can handle that.

On Wednesday evening, I reach the coffee shop a few minutes before seven, but Jordie's already here. He's seated at the same table he and his teammates were at the night of the book club meeting. I recall him sitting there last time wearing a pink polo shirt, a cup of coffee in front of him, his cocky smile on full display when I approached the table.

This time, things are different. His expression is somber, and he looks tired. His hair is sticking up in a few different directions, like he's been running his fingers through it, and his jaw is unshaven.

As I lower myself into the chair across from him, Jordie's gaze snaps up to mine.

"Harper." My name leaves his lips in a deep rush.

"Hey." My voice is barely above a whisper.

"How are you?" he asks, his low voice making my heart give a painful kick.

I duck my head, considering his question. Deciding it's a cursory question, I won't overthink it. "I've been okay," I say cautiously.

"That's good." There's a pregnant pause, a moment of silence between us, and then Jordie leans closer. "Did you read it?"

"I did," I say, keeping my voice neutral.

He nods once and licks his lips. "Can I get you anything to drink? Coffee? Tea?"

I shake my head. "I'm good."

He swallows. "Right. Well, thanks for coming. I just . . . wanted to apologize in person. See how you're feeling."

How I'm feeling? Is he serious right now? I'm barely hanging on. Although we weren't together long, what we had was real to me. And now that it's over, I feel lost and broken.

"Oh, ya know . . ." I smirk, blinking back the tears that fill my eyes.

He curses low under his breath and clenches one fist on the table. "I can't keep doing this. Can't keep pretending I'm okay . . ."

"Why not?"

His eyes meet mine. "Because I'm in love with you, Harper."

My heart stops. I press my fingers to my lips as my gaze searches his. I need to know if he's telling the truth, and what I see reflected back at me almost levels me. There's so much emotion in his dark blue eyes.

"You lied about the bet, and hid that from me the whole time we knew each other. How do I know you're not lying about this?" My voice sounds composed, thank God, and yet I feel anything but. In fact, my hands are shaking so badly, I have to place them in my lap.

"I love how smart you are."

"Jor—"

"I love that you hate hockey players."

"Jordie—"

"I love that when you're happy, all you want to do is eat sugary breakfast foods. I love that you're so focused on your career. I love how stubborn you are, and that most of the time, you're right. I love the way your eyelids flutter open when you wake up in the morning, and I love that you can't sleep without the fan on at night. I love you, Harper Allen. I'm *in* love with you. And I think you love me too. I'll be damned if I let one asshole mistake I made keep us from exploring what we have."

Absolutely stunned, I look down at my hands,

my mouth open. Part of me can't believe he's laying it all out on the table. I guess I expected him to be guarded, or play some kind of game. But Jordie never does what I expect him to.

"Say something. Please," he says low, and his voice cracks.

"I don't know what to say. I don't know if I'll only be hurt again if I forgive you . . ."

"You won't," he says quickly.

"I miss you," I say softly as a single tear rolls down my cheek.

"God, Harper." His voice is a breathless rasp. "I miss you so fucking much."

I give him a sad smile.

Jordie reaches for my hand and curls his palm around mine. "Can we go someplace private and talk?"

CHAPTER TWENTY-FOUR

And They Both Lived . . .

Harper

"Okay, I think that's the last of them," I call out, watching Jordie and a couple of his muscular teammates haul the last three cardboard boxes over the threshold of his apartment.

Sorry, let me rephrase that. *Our* apartment. Any minute now, I feel like someone's going to pinch me, and I'll find out all this is just part of my craziest, wildest, happiest dream.

Jordie sets the box on the floor with a grunt and stands, his chest heaving, sweat glistening on his forehead. I'm not mad about what a little perspiration is doing to the fit of his T-shirt. I can't believe *this*—the abs, the biceps, the blue eyes, the big heart—all of it, all of *him*, is mine.

"I think I saw a freight truck exiting the freeway. Are you sure it's not yours?" he asks between panted breaths, his brow scrunched.

"Are you a little out of shape, rookie?" I tease, closing the distance between us to gaze up at him. He smells like male and deodorant, an intoxicating mixture that makes me wish his teammates could evaporate with a snap of my fingers.

He smiles and tips his face toward mine. "You've got a lot of shit, Harp. And it's heavy."

I lean in even closer. Our mouths are only inches apart now, and the tension between us is like a rope pulling taut, right before it snaps in two. When the next words leave my lips, I forget we're not the only two people in the room.

"Maybe it's time we really get that heart rate going."

Justin and Teddy exchange a look. When they open their mouths, they speak at the same time.

Teddy says, "We should probably . . ."

Just as Justin blurts, "Yeah, I've got to get back to Elise."

The four of us laugh, and Jordie steps away to give them a couple of bro hugs, slapping their backs and thanking them for helping. But what Jordie and I just started is nowhere near over.

"I appreciate it, guys," he says, sliding an arm around my waist as we walk them to the door. *Our* door. I'm still getting used to that.

"Don't mention it," Teddy says. "And, hey, congrats, you two. I'm really happy you were able to work it out. We were pulling for you."

"Yeah, and just remember—no matter how tense things get, the make-up sex? Always worth it," Justin says, dodging one last punch in the arm from Jordie.

We close the door and turn around to take in our new living room. Boxes are stacked in piles on the floor, all with handwritten labels like HARPER'S BATHROOM, HARPER'S KITCHEN TOOLS, HARPER'S SLOW COOKER. My three suitcases are waiting to be unpacked in the bedroom, and I've already spent a good chunk of the day hanging clothes on my side of the closet.

All at once, reality truly sinks in, and I loop my arm around Jordie's waist and lay my head on his chest.

"I live here now," I murmur.

He wraps his arm across my shoulders and

pulls me closer. "This is the start of our forever."

A warm, melty feeling spreads from my chest down to my toes. Staying here, like this, in Jordie's arms forever? I like the sound of that.

We start sorting the boxes, putting the kitchen stuff in the kitchen, the bathroom stuff over by the bathroom, the living room decor in the living room, etc. It's the kind of work that would be tedious, but given the excitement bubbling underneath the surface of everything I do today, this might as well be the damn Stanley Cup finals.

"Hey, uh, Harp?" Jordie calls from the hallway.

"Yeah, babe?"

Babe. The word rolls off my tongue, sweet and easy, like I've been calling him that my whole life. Am I even a "babe" girl? Maybe I'm more of a "honey" kind of girl. Or maybe "sweetie"? Darling? Hot cheeks? Bae?

I'll know it when I hear myself say it.

He appears in the living room with a medium-sized box in his arms. "Where's all this go?"

He offers the open box, and I peer inside to find a bunch of framed photos of various sizes. I carefully sort through them. Photos of my sister and me, of my dad, of our family on Faith's wedding day, of my nieces. Each photo makes my heart swell a little more.

"They were all hanging in my bedroom. Don't you remember?"

The corner of his mouth pulls into a smile. "I was a little focused on *other things* when I was in your bedroom," he says, and I don't miss the hungry look that flashes in his eyes.

I smile and shake my head, laying the frames gently back into the box. "These can go in the bedroom."

He looks at me quizzically. "They can?"

"That's where they go."

"My room's not exactly—"

"*Our* room." I cut him off, my eyebrows raised expectantly.

"Our room," he says slowly, "isn't really a *hang your family photos and string Christmas lights across the wall* kind of bedroom."

"Who said anything about Christmas lights?"

He rummages below the frames in the box, pulls out a small string of twinkle lights, and holds them in front of his face.

"Those were strung around my bathroom mirror," I say, snatching them out of his hands.

"Apparently, I only ever used your bathroom with the lights off," he mutters, confusion written all over his face.

"Remind me why we can't hang photos in our bedroom?"

"The walls have a Roman clay finish."

"A what?"

"I'm not paying for the cost of labor twice."

I stare at him blankly. "I feel like I don't even know you right now."

He shrugs, sets the box down in the living room, and stands in front of the couch. "What about this wall?"

"You mean the one perpendicular to the stunning view of the water?"

"I mean the one in the living room, the homiest room in the house. That's where the photos of your family go."

"Our bedroom's not homey?"

He pulls me in for a hug and we stare at the wall together, my head against his chest. It's like this is our new default.

"I don't think I can handle having Coach in the bedroom," he murmurs into my hair.

Oh. I giggle. "Yeah, I guess it's time to stop throwing a handkerchief over his photo to protect his innocence."

We laugh, and Jordie holds me tighter.

Everything about this feels right. His arms around me, the two of us squabbling about interior decorating, all of it. These are the things couples do. That *we* do. And I'm just so damn happy we found each other and worked it all out.

My stomach growls loudly, cutting through our contented silence.

I laugh again, and Jordie grins down at me.

"Sounds like it's time to break for dinner."

We walk to the kitchen, where I lean against the cool granite counter, racking my brain for what sounds good. "Should we pick something up, or . . ."

Jordie shakes his head, pulling a cab from the

wine rack and two glasses from the shelf. A sneaky little grin forms on his lips. God, he's sexy. If he keeps that up, I'll forget about dinner completely.

"I had something else in mind," he says, uncorking the wine and pouring us each a glass. "Let me make you dinner. Like I did on our first date."

He slides a glass across the counter, and I take it, cocking my head to the side.

"It wasn't a date," I say, arching a challenging brow.

"Harper, I made you spaghetti. I saved the day. We shared a killer kiss. Now, doesn't that sound an awful lot like a date to you?" He gathers the ingredients for our meal as he talks, that same playful, sexy grin on his face.

Was it always this difficult to disagree with him? I raise my eyebrows and cross my arms, but I don't respond—mostly because I can't think of anything to say. He's got a point.

Jordie shrugs and continues with a sigh. "I guess what I'm trying to say is that it was real for me. Whatever you might have been feeling."

My heart doesn't melt this time. It vaporizes.

"I'd be lying if I said I didn't have feelings for

you then too." I place my hand over his, and he smiles.

"So, what do you say? Can I make you dinner?"

"Why don't I help this time? We're on the same team now. We work together."

We kiss, and his mouth tastes slightly fruity and oaky from the wine.

After everything we've been through—our rocky beginning, the heartbreak—to be here with him now, ready to start this new chapter together? It's magic. Nothing else that's happened between us matters. All that matters is the fact that we're here, that we're choosing today, and each other, and this life. I wouldn't trade any of it.

"All right then, *teammate*, you can get started on boiling water," he says, nodding to one of the large pots hanging above the stove.

"Are you doubting my ability to cook as well as you?" I lower the pot and begin filling it at the sink, watching the water slowly rise.

"A team's only as strong as its weakest link," he says when he returns from the pantry, pasta and tomatoes in hand.

"Oh, you are so going down, Jordie Prescott."

I grab the sink sprayer and aim for his face. He dodges just in time, and most of the water lands on the floor behind him, but the look on his face suggests otherwise. It's filled with surprise.

He drops the food on the counter and rounds the corner toward me, so I aim the sprayer at him again. This time I hit my target, and within seconds, Jordie's whole front is drenched.

We both laugh as he wipes the water from his eyes, his T-shirt plastered to his chest.

"That's it," he says, his lip curling into a smile. "Into the shower. Both of us."

"What?"

Before I can comprehend what's about to happen, he picks me up by my waist and throws me over his shoulder, then marches us down the hallway and into the bathroom.

"You were saying something earlier about getting my heart rate going?" he says, flipping the light switch and setting me on the edge of the counter.

That same rope of tension pulls taut between us as he centers himself between my knees, the steam from the shower already starting to rise.

"I think I've got a few ideas."

EPILOGUE

Jordie

Several months later . . .

This is insane.

"Is this real life?" Harper stands beside me with a wide-eyed expression.

"It is for us, baby."

Her hand finds mine, and she gives it a squeeze.

We spent the morning flying across the country. Seattle to Atlanta, Atlanta to Saint Maarten, and then a ferry from Saint Maarten to the island of Anguilla.

Several members of the team are here, either as guests of Justin and Elise's wedding, like Harper and I are, or as members of the wedding party, like Grant, Owen, Teddy, and Asher, plus their significant others. Justin and Elise's families are due to arrive on the island tomorrow.

After we disembark from the ferry, we're greeted by the sight of white sandy beaches and little pastel-colored buildings. A driver waits, ready to take us and our luggage to the property Justin and Elise have rented for the week.

I take Harper's rolling suitcase from her and help the driver place all our luggage into the back of the SUV.

After we ended our season by abruptly getting pushed out of the playoffs by New York, I'm in need of a little rest and relaxation. On the wedding itinerary I received via email, a spa day is planned for the girls and a poker tournament for the guys. There's a shipwreck to explore and snorkeling to be done. It's a good thing I like my teammates, otherwise this would be *a lot* of team-bonding time.

On the drive to our home for the next week, Harper alternates looking out the windows at our surroundings—which is mostly jungle—and reading something on her phone.

I peek over her shoulder and see she's reading an article titled HOW TO AVOID BEING AN OBNOXIOUS TOURIST IN ANGUILLA.

I chuckle and raise a brow at her. "Why are you reading that?" Harper's the least obnoxious person I've ever met, tourist or not. She's respectful and considerate.

"Are you kidding? I've read everything I can get my hands on about Anguilla. I may never go on a vacation this fancy ever again. I've read every blog post, and every restaurant review. I know the best beaches, the unsafe areas to avoid—everything."

I give her a confused look. "I guess I forgot how much you like to read."

She nods. "Never underestimate my love of reading."

"I won't, baby." I pat her bare knee.

When we arrive, all my expectations are blown out of the water. Even calm-and-collected Harper lets out a shocked gasp from beside me.

"This is stunning," she says, taking everything in as we climb from our ride.

I knew the property would be impressive, but this is next level. It's a private oasis with a large main house where the bride and groom will stay, and then smaller cottages, each with one or two bedrooms, dotting the cliffside property. I'm sure it's costing him upward of a hundred thousand dollars a night, but I guess money is of little consequence when you make as much of it as Justin Brady does.

And for the next week, there will be white sandy beaches, crystal-clear turquoise water, and secluded coves to explore. I have a week of sun and serenity and Harper. I'm a happy man.

"Let's go see who's here," Harper says as I tip the driver.

"Lead the way." I leave the bags by the huge glass front door, and we let ourselves inside.

"Hello?" Harper calls.

I wonder if she's thinking the same thing I am—that we don't want to accidentally interrupt anything if Justin and Elise are here alone and feeling frisky before they say *I do*. But then we hear male laughter coming from upstairs, and Harper and I share a relieved look.

"What the fuck, Brady?" Owen's deep voice rumbles out the words, but it's followed by a bark of laughter, from Justin, I think.

"Put a dollar in the swear jar!" Becca says,

chastising her husband.

When Harper and I reach the top of the stairs, we see that most of the crew is here, playing a boisterous game of Ping-Pong, of all things.

Elise rushes over to wrap Harper in a hug. Becca, carrying her son, Bishop, on one hip does the same. I greet Grant with a handshake and give Ana a one-armed hug. The firm, round bump of her stomach presses against my side. It's strange.

I grin down at her. "You feeling okay?"

She nods. "Never better." Their daughter, Hunter, is playing with a foam hockey puck on the floor.

Harper and I say our hellos to everyone, and Elise offers us a beer. We both accept and head to the sectional to watch the next Ping-Pong match-up, which is between newlyweds Teddy and Sara. Since there's nowhere for both of us to sit comfortably, I pull Harper into my lap. She gives me a sly grin but settles in against me, quietly sipping her beer.

I try to watch the game and even throw in some trash talk of my own, but the soft weight of Harper's ass against my groin is more than a little distracting. My cock starts to stir, which is unfortunate, given that I'm wearing linen shorts that will do fuck-all to hide that fact.

With a furrowed brow, Harper turns and gives me a look. "Really, Prescott?"

A deep rumble of laughter leaves my lips. *God, this woman.* I take a deep breath and try to wrangle my dick under control. It helps only marginally.

"Ready to see our cottage?" I ask with a sly grin.

"Sure." Harper hops up and gives my crotch a cursory glance.

I shake my head. "We're gonna go explore," I say to no one in particular, rising to my feet.

Elise gives Harper another hug, along with directions to our cottage, which is three doors over. According to Elise, it's the bungalow with the hammock on the front porch.

Harper leads the way down the stone walkway while I pull our rolling suitcases behind me.

"Wow," is the first word out of her mouth when she opens the front door to the cottage, which is quaint but luxurious.

Large picture windows let in plenty of light. As we make our way through the living room, with its tile floors and heavy wooden furniture, I leave the suitcases where they are, noting the colorful art on the walls. Inside the bedroom, a king-size bed is dressed in fluffy white bedding, and in the en-suite bathroom is a rain shower and a large freestanding tub. Beyond is a sun-drenched outdoor terrace with a private plunge pool.

Wow is right. I wasn't expecting that. I can't help but wonder if Justin hooked me up with the best accommodations because of the question I told him I plan to pop on this trip. Either way, this place is romantic as fuck.

"This is amazing," Harper says with a laugh, standing by the sliding glass doors in the bedroom that lead out to the private terrace.

I pause behind her and gather her in my arms. Harper leans back against me and lets out a happy sigh. My cock twitches, hardening again.

She turns slowly until she's facing me. "You seem to be having a problem today."

If that problem is keeping my dick flaccid anytime her body comes into contact with mine, then yes, I'm having a problem.

I give her a cocky grin. "You offering up a solution?"

With a cocky smile of her own, Harper drops to her knees right there on the bedroom floor. And before I can formulate a response, her fingers are working open the front of my shorts.

I'm fully hard when I take myself in my hand and stroke. Harper kisses a hot path along my aching shaft. When her lips close around me, I make an inarticulate sound, and the muscles in my stomach tighten.

"Baby," I say on a groan. "*Fuck*. That feels good."

She treats the head of my cock to a slow, wet kiss with plenty of suction, and I hiss out a string of curses. The sight of her on her knees before me is the most erotic thing I've ever seen, and a bolt of heat flashes down my spine.

"Deeper," I say, swallowing another groan.

I want her to keep going, but I also know I should stop her before things get too far. But *fuuuck*. It feels so good. The girl has serious skills, but the chance to watch her come on my cock wins out.

"Need you to stop doing that," I rasp out.

With a wicked look, she eases back and traces

her tongue over my swollen tip. "You sure about that?"

I'm not even sure I could spell my own damn name at this point, but I nod. "I want to be inside you." I curl one fist around my cock and remove it from her mouth—which I pretty much deserve a medal for.

"Get on the bed," I say in a rough voice.

While Harper scrambles onto the mattress and begins stripping off her clothing, I stand next to the bed and slowly stroke myself. Her lips part on a shaky exhale as she watches me.

"Come here." She kicks off her underwear and reaches for me.

I join her on the bed, kissing and licking all of my favorite places on her body—her mouth, her soft breasts, the dip in her stomach—before I settle between her legs. With soft strokes of my tongue, I tease and kiss, but Harper shifts restlessly beneath me.

"Please," she says, tugging me up. "I'm already close, and I want you inside me when I come."

I can't argue with her logic, so I position my-self on top of her, kissing her neck, her forehead, her lips. I'm not sure if it's impatience or just desire, but Harper can't wait any longer. She takes me in her hand and lines us up. When I press forward, we both let out a ragged groan.

Oh fuck, that feels good.

Her lips part, and my name slips out in a whisper. The sound makes my heart clench.

I find a steady, even rhythm that makes Harper shiver, and I keep fucking her just like that until she comes apart, shaking in my arms and moaning out her relief.

"Love you," I whisper. "So much."

"Me too," she rasps, out of breath.

Her fingers latch onto my hair, and she tugs. Some garbled word comes out of her mouth the second time she comes—it might be my name. I'm not sure.

I brace myself above her, stroking her cheek with the rough pad of my thumb while I push myself deep inside her.

Chasing my own release now, I pump faster and press my mouth to hers. Harper kisses me as I fall over the edge. My release pulses out of me in wave after hot wave, and breathlessly, I roll to my side, tugging her on top of me.

As she nestles in close, I bring my arms around her. "Sorry. I swear I didn't mean to maul you as soon as we got here."

With a soft chuckle, Harper brings her mouth to mine for a quick kiss. "I wasn't complaining."

We lie there together as our heart rates slow, and just the feel of her in my arms is something I'll never take for granted again. Those weeks when I thought I'd lost her was the hardest time of my life.

The thought that I could have gone my whole life and never had this is a sobering one. Now that I've found Harper, I'm never letting her go. And the best news is, we have all week to enjoy each other like this.

The next morning, between sips of coffee and bites of toasted bagels, she tells me about a book idea that came to her while she slept last night.

I listen as she animatedly describes the entire plot. Grinning, I remember that time I mentioned to her someone should write a romance novel about a hockey player. That someone is going to be Harper.

"I'll be your muse," I say with a smirk.

She laughs and shakes her head. "That could

be fun."

• • •

Justin and Elise's wedding was the most low-key ceremony I've ever been to.

At sunset, they exchanged rings on the beach, barefoot, surrounded by about two dozen people. There were heartfelt vows, along with a few laughs, and then Justin lifted his new wife in his arms and kissed the daylights out of her.

This got a grumble out of her brother, Owen, but everyone knew he was kidding. Justin treats Elise like a queen, and so even if them dating was a *thing* at first between the guys, it certainly isn't now.

The reception is just as casual. Reggae music. Delicious seafood. Harper beside me.

And . . . the weight of a ring box in my pocket. It seems surreal, but there's no one else I'd rather spend my life with.

As I look around at my teammates and friends, it's hard not to notice what I lucky bastard I am. Justin and Elise are now happily married and swaying together on a sandy dance floor under the stars. Owen and Becca are married with a kid—a sleeping kid who's passed out on his dad's shoulder at the moment. Grant and Ana, who are also married and have a toddler and another baby on the way. Teddy and Sara—happily married and sharing a slice of cake. Morgan and his girlfriend, Isla, are dancing too. My old teammate Landon, who was traded to Vancouver a season ago, and his wife, Aubree, are here, as happy and in love as I've ever seen them, and there's been talk about them adopting a baby. Asher and Bailey, who are now pregnant and engaged to be married next month.

And Harper and I could be next.

I take Harper's hand. "Come walk with me?"

"But it's dark. And why leave the party?" She gives me a questioning look.

"Just walk with me." I tip my chin toward the darkened beach. "Please."

"Fine. But you're being weird."

I chuckle. "Just come on. I'll make it worth your while."

The sand is like powdered sugar beneath our feet, turning to soft clay when the waves rush over it. Harper lets out a little squeal and holds up the hem of her gauzy lavender dress. We walk hand in hand for a little while until the sounds of laughter and music are far behind us.

"It was a beautiful wedding," Harper says into the darkness.

"Yeah. It was. Is this something you'd like . . . a destination wedding?"

She looks over, briefly meeting my eyes. "You really want to know?"

"Of course I do."

A smile crosses her lips. "I think I would. It's more than just a wedding. It's a vacation for all your friends and family. Lots of good memories, you know?"

I nod. "That's true."

We walk a little farther, and then I pause and turn Harper toward me. My stomach erupts with nerves, but when I meet her eyes, I feel instantly calm.

"Hey," I say, flashing her an uneven smile.

She gives me a confused look. "Hey?"

I swallow. *Jesus, I'm messing this up already.* With a deep inhale, I force myself to relax and re-member the words I wrote out in my journal last week in preparation for this moment.

"I love you. And I . . . have something I want to ask you."

Harper's eyes widen as I pull the ring box from my pocket. When her gaze darts to mine, I see every emotion she's feeling. Excitement. Disbelief. Anticipation.

I sink down to one knee right there on the sand. Still holding Harper's hand, I press a soft kiss to the back of it.

"I know I wasn't always the best boyfriend. But being with you has taught me so much. And I hope to get to prove to you just how much I love you . . . for the rest of forever."

"Jordie . . ." Harper's voice is tight with emotion, and a single tear slips down her cheek.

I'm barely holding my own emotions in check. My voice low and raspy, I say, "Baby, will you marry me?"

"Oh God, Jordie. Yes!" she cries. "I love you. Yes."

I rise to my feet and lift Harper into my arms. Tears are freely streaming down her cheeks now, and I kiss each one away.

I slip the ring onto Harper's trembling finger, and she gasps. Not gonna lie, I did a damn good job picking out this ring. I even consulted her sister to find out what style Harper would like, and picked out an oval solitaire diamond surrounded by rubies. It's unique and beautiful, just like Harper.

Once the ring is securely on her finger, Harper meets my eyes. With one finger under her chin, I tilt her mouth to mine. Our kiss is slow, lingering, and unhurried, but the simmering attraction that burns just below the surface is already threatening to erupt. I can't wait to be alone with her later.

"The future Mrs. Harper Prescott," I whisper against her lips. "Unless you're planning to keep your name?"

She smiles, her eyes glittering. "I would be proud to be Harper Prescott."

"I wish my dad could be here to meet you, to share this with us," I say softly. Dad would have loved Harper, and would have welcomed her into the family with open arms.

"He will always be here with us. I love hearing stories about him, and one day when we have babies, I want us to tell them all about their grandpa in heaven."

My heart gives another thump as my emotions threaten to spill out. I squeeze my eyes shut and hold her close.

We begin the walk back toward the wedding reception, and when we get about halfway there, Harper stops suddenly.

"Oh God, we can't tell anyone. We're going to ruin their wedding day." She gasps, staring back at me with worry-filled eyes.

"Huh?"

She nods. "Elise and Justin are supposed to be the center of attention today. Not us. Seriously, Jordie. We'd better not say anything tonight."

I turn her by the shoulders to face me and press a kiss to her lips. "Everyone already knew I was going to propose. Justin and Elise. The whole team. Your dad. Your sister. Everyone."

She smiles. "They did?"

I nod. "I kinda sucked at keeping it a secret. Even my dry-cleaning person saw your ring. Shit, I think I showed the grocery store clerk too last week."

She laughs. "Oh. Well, in that case."

I pull her tight against me and steal another kiss.

Harper pulls back and looks down at her ring, which glimmers in the moonlight. "But what if I hadn't said yes?"

I shudder. "That wasn't a possibility I let myself think about."

She nods. "Probably wise. But there was absolutely no way I wasn't going to say yes. I love you so freaking much."

"You're stuck with me now, baby."

With another soft smile, Harper laces her fingers through mine. "There's no place else I'd rather be."

My heart gives one more happy lurch, as we head back toward the party to share our good news with our friends.

It's in that moment that I know. Even if Harper never gets around to writing her novel, I know without a doubt that she's the heroine in my story. And I've got the best happily-ever-after that's ever been written.

Ours.

HAVE YOU MET ALL THE HOT JOCKS YET?

Hot Jocks Series Reading Order

Playing for Keeps – Justin and Elise

All the Way – Becca and Owen

Trying to Score – Teddy and Sara

Crossing the Line – Asher and Bailey

The Bedroom Experiment – Morgan and Isla – a spin-off novelette

Down and Dirty – Landon and Aubree

Wild for You – Grant and Ana

Taking His Shot – Jordie and Harper

ACKNOWLEDGMENTS

A heartfelt thank-you to all the lovely readers who have followed this series from book one, *Playing for Keeps*, until now. It's been quite a journey! This series really consumed me (in a good way), and each book presented a unique challenge—to capture the new characters' voices, but also remain true to the tone of the series, and to bring back fan favorites while not letting them take over the story. I'm sad that it's all coming to an end, but I fully believe in writing a second hockey series at some point in the future. So we all have that to look forward to. Yay!

I have so much gratitude for the amazing women on my team who help me get through. Alyssa Garcia, I'm thankful for everything you do. You are a godsend! Pam Berehulke, your editing magic is really beyond, and yet it's virtually stress-free working with you, which again, seems like it takes a bit of magic. Rachel Brookes, I'm blessed to have you in my corner, keeping my secrets and sharing in my triumphs. Thank you, girl, for having my back. Onward, always.

Stacy Garcia, what can I say, other than thank you! Oh, and Noah says hi.

Thank you, bloggers, big and small for all you do! Thanks to Lyric Audio for producing my audio-books. Thank you also to all the authors who have been along for the ride . . . Nana Malone, Sarina Bowen, Monica Murphy, Elle Kennedy, Lexi Ryan, Erin Nicholas, Helena Hunting, Jan Scott, Avery Flynn, Kelly Elliott, and Monica James. I have so much love and respect for all of you. Thank you for your help, kind thoughts, or lending me your ear during my publishing journey with this series.

WHAT TO READ NEXT...
HOW TO D♡TE
A *Younger* MAN

If you accidentally bang your best friend's younger brother, here are a few important tips . . .

One: Do *not* brag to your friend about how well-endowed her brother is.

Two: Do not go back for seconds (or thirds).

Three: Do not let him see your muffin top or jiggly behind. And definitely don't let him feed you cookies in bed. Cookies are bad. Remember that.

Four: Act like a damn grown-up and apologize for riding him like a bull at the rodeo. And *do not* flirt with him when he laughs at said apology.

Five: This one is crucial, so pay attention.

Do *not*, under any circumstances, fall in love with him.

Made in the USA
Las Vegas, NV
18 December 2021

38580873R00204